Lala Richardson Fisher

By Creek and Gully

stories and sketches mostly of bush life - Told in prose and rhyme

Lala Richardson Fisher

By Creek and Gully
stories and sketches mostly of bush life - Told in prose and rhyme

ISBN/EAN: 9783337260408

Printed in Europe, USA, Canada, Australia, Japan

Cover: Foto ©Andreas Hilbeck / pixelio.de

More available books at **www.hansebooks.com**

MARGARET THOMAS. + OLIPHANT SMEATON. + E. S. RAWSON. + HON. PEMBER REEVES. + E. W. HORNUNG.

+ LALA FISHER. + LOUIS BECKE. + HUME NISBET. +

By
Creek and Gully

Stories and Sketches mostly of Bush
Life. Told in Prose and Rhyme.
By Australian Writers in
England. Edited by
Lala Fisher

London

T. FISHER UNWIN

MDCCCXCIX

+ DOUGLAS SLADEN. + MRS. CAFFYN. + JOHN ELKIN. +

MRS. CAMPBELL PRAED. + FRANK RICHARDSON. + MRS. PATCHETT MARTIN. + H. B. MARRIOTT WATSON.

To

W. KNOX D'ARCY, ESQ.,

OF

STANMORE HALL,

THIS BOOK IS AFFECTIONATELY DEDICATED.

CONTENTS

CONTENTS

TO THE STORY-MAKERS

BY LALA FISHER

TO THE STORY-MAKERS

BY LALA FISHER

WHEN fairies weave a wizard spell,
   And conjure up before our eyes
The days and scenes we loved so well,
   And men and maids long lost arise—
When at their bidding camp-fires gleam
   With boiling billy on the hook,
It seems so true and sweet a dream
   The gazer nearer draws to look.

Up with the sun, we paddocks pass,
   Where lazy bullocks lift their heaas
To see us go, then crop the grass
   That grows beside the dry creek-beds.
The stock-whip coils upon our knee,
   Our pannikin is strapped behind;
We ride across the wakening lea
   The lost and straying beasts to find.

The wary kangaroos close by
   Are browsing when our nags draw near;
Alarmed, they to their joeys fly,
   Who in a twinkling disappear—

Disdaining haste—with measured bounds
 They vanish o'er the distant hill;
We whistle back the eager dogs
 So thirsty to pursue and kill.

Once more the crystal creek we breast,
 Showering its pearl-drops high in air;
We part the rushes, see a nest
 Of ducklings golden hidden there!
While fairy fish in glittering flocks
 Dart o'er the pebbles blue and red,
A kukaburra laughs and mocks,
 Safe in a gum-tree overhead.

Now slowly forging up the track
 The tirèd musterer returns;
His hanging head and bended back
 Above his horse one scarce discerns.
His idle reins no touch await
 To guide or check the patient steed,
Who stops beside the homestead gate
 To pull a switch of swamp-grown feed.

Then over all a tender light
 Slow settles as the sunlight dies:
The tree-tops catch its misty white
 Ere yet upon the land it lies;
The flowers know it and are glad,
 The breezes meet it with a sigh,
The bushman sees it and grows sad
 And thoughtful, though he recks not why.

'Tis night! how still the bush has grown,
  With sentinels of ring-barked trees;
The ghostly stars give light alone,
  And mournful whispers fill each breeze!
A lonely 'possum steals along
  And lightly passes to its nest,
A sleepy mopoke drones a song,
  Then the vast land sinks into rest.

A magic power indeed ye hold
  Who wield the sweet, enchanted pen;
To more old hearts than could be told
  Thou bringest back life's youth again!
Beneath thy thrall hopes blossom fair,
  The soul's regret forgotten lies,
With lagging wings afar flies Care,
  And Joy beams forth from happy eyes!

CROSS CURRENTS

BY MRS. PATCHETT MARTIN

CROSS CURRENTS

BY MRS. PATCHETT MARTIN

I

A HALT BY THE RIVER

WHEN Alma Belmont arrived at Bristowe she had done about as foolish a thing as any young woman of four-and-twenty could have done in the way of marring a life that had been only too pleasant. Spoilt as a child, indulged in her wilful, wayward fancies as the only daughter of a long-widowed parent, much petted and admired in the set in which she moved, she had elected to consider herself an ill-used and unhappy creature, and had impulsively and hurriedly married a man who had come to her one day with a plea to " save him from going to the devil, for she was about the only woman who could do it."

The excuse she made to the world was her father's second marriage; to herself the impossibility of marrying the "only man she had ever really loved," and a kind of pride in the thought of reclaiming a poor fellow who loved her from the error of his ways. She was able to impose upon herself perhaps more successfully than on other people, who failed to see that a rich stepmother who "entertained," and did her duty by society and marriageable maidens, was other than a highly estimable person, or that, as far as Alma herself was concerned, her devotion to a girlish ideal had ever stood in the way of many flirtations and a very patent enjoyment of her ballroom triumphs and successes.   As to reclaiming Captain Belmont, the utter fallacy of such an aspiration revealed itself to her in the early days of her marriage, which were spent on board ship on their outward voyage to Australia.

He was one of those gentlemanly and agreeable ne'er-do-weels whom other men characterise as " no man's enemy but his own," who had a " taking " way with women, much superficial good-nature, and an utter absence of principle.   Withal, not destitute of a certain kind of cleverness, and possessed of a winning, almost boyish, affectionateness, which made his own womankind very gentle and tender and forgiving towards him, until came those evil days when he had sunk so low that even they could forgive and tolerate him no longer.

It is not, however, the story of Alma Belmont's married life that I have to tell, though it would have furnished material for a three-volume novel, but merely to relate an episode which did not even indirectly concern her husband, who had gone " up country " at the time in quest of one of those vague and frequently mythical " appointments " which he was very fond or talking about, and which entailed much acceptance or hospitality and even of monetary loans from genial hosts and open-handed Australian acquaintances, whom the plausible and quick-witted Irishman won over by his gift of ready speech and the inventive powers that never failed him.

On this occasion, however, the "appointment," which was "something in the Customs," was genuine, and Alma Belmont was on her way to the northern town of Stony Hollow to join her husband, who had preceded her, and who was staying there with a relative holding a position under Government.

Stony Hollow was reached by a three days' sea and river journey from the capital, from whence the high Customs official, who had held out a helping hand to the young couple, had seen Alma on board the steamer, with the kindly information that he had requested his brother collector at Ellenborough, where the vessel stopped for a night to take in and discharge cargo, to find her out on board, and thus make a break in the loneliness of her solitary journey.

It was in summer time, and every mile that they sped northward but increased the stifling heat and discomfort of the passage. It had been rough in the bay, there were even waves in the big river, and Alma had been seasick and was very miserable.

A wretched little six-weeks-old kitten, which her husband had requested her to bring for his cousin's children, had added to her misery by its piteous refusal to drink milk that had turned sour, and she was every moment expecting the poor little thing would die in the stuffy basket in which she had brought it so far at much personal inconvenience. The premature demise of a baby kitten may not seem a trouble to distress one's self about; but the lonely young wife was in that condition of forlornness that she had almost grown to care for her little travelling companion, and the stewardess's openly-expressed opinion that she couldn't think how any one could have troubled themselves with a "common little tabby kitten" quite grated upon her feelings.

She had been reviewing in her mind all the circumstances that had attended her short stay in the colony; how they had landed with no possessions beyond the clothing in their boxes and a ten-pound note, half of which had gone to pay the laundress for washing the linen that had accumulated during the hundred days of their long journey in a sailing ship. She dwelt on the dismay with which she had contemplated the plethoric linen-bag and the attenuated purse, and the joyful surprise with which she had accepted a kindly hospitality proffered "until they could turn themselves round, and Captain Belmont should find something to do."

They had not only "turned themselves round" pretty frequently in the pleasant riverside home of their kind entertainers, but had even gyrated in the viceregal precincts, and assisted at balls and receptions at Government House, where Captain Belmont's waltzing and Mrs. Belmont's pretty French frocks had come in for a fair share of admiration. Several things had been found for Captain Belmont to do, but his doings had been of a perfunctory nature, and the illegible scrawl on which he rather prided himself had not advanced his position in the Government office which he had honoured with a trial. "Set of scribbling cads!" was his remark to his wife. "Ought to think themselves d——d lucky to have a gentleman amongst them."

Alma did not feel very sanguine as to the appointment in the Customs, and she was looking forward with nervous dread of the unknown life to which she was going, the unknown connections whose house they were to share, and the very slight prospect of any permanent home of their own being ever provided for her. She was tired of living with or upon other people, and this shuttlecock state of existence was highly distasteful to her. Stony Hollow, too, from all accounts, was not exactly the place one would select for a residence in summer, being built down in a basin and surrounded by a range of low hills, which were quite high enough to exclude all air from the dwellers in its midst. So her musings were not of a very pleasant nature as she sat alone in her deck chair watching the sunset until it grew dark with the sudden darkness of a sky that has no twilight. Cockroaches were beginning to issue forth from the nooks and crannies in which they had lain concealed during the day, and as the ship made its way up the river through narrowing banks, on which the dismal mangrove grew thickly, the large spotted mosquito which haunts these shores deserted the accursed shrub that gives it shelter to settle about the ship and on its sweltering denizens.

They were nearing Ellenborough, where a halt was to be made during the night to discharge and take in cargo, the new goldfields that had lately been discovered a few miles from the township having given it a commercial impetus which warranted the delay, even in the case of a vessel that called itself a passenger steamer. They had now reached the landing-stage; ropes had been made fast to the piles with the usual accompaniment of "Heave away!" "Hold fast there!"

and "aye ayeing;" and the Custom House officials were stepping on board. Amongst them was a tall, slender lad with a profusion of brown curls tumbling out from under his straw hat, who accosted the captain, and to Alma's astonishment at once asked if "Mrs. Belmont was on board." When directed by a wave of the hand towards the lady in question, he came straight up to her, and as he raised his hat with a courteous gesture, introduced himself as "Athanase Bingham."

"My father, you know, is the Collector of Customs here, and Mr. Thornhill, of Bristowe, asked him to look you up. My mother charged me to bring you to the house to supper, and to say that you must not think of going back to the steamer to-night, as there is a bed at your disposal."

"Indeed, I shall be only too glad," responded Alma, hastily adjusting the small toque she wore, and rising from her chair to follow her young visitor, who carefully assisted her to land, walking some distance along the quay and leading the way through a small gate that opened to the wharf, from an enclosure in which stood the Custom House. Passing one side of the building, and along the wall of a covered passage that seemed to connect it with a low, one-storied, verandahed dwelling-house, they found themselves in a garden, through which they passed, entering the house through a broad French window opening out on the verandah into a large, untidy, and yet comfortable-looking room, that revealed the harmonious life of a family by its combined masculine, feminine, and boyish litter. It was imperfectly lit by a lamp on a centre table, and at first Alma could but dimly discern the figure belonging to a rich voice that greeted her in foreign accents.

"Be welcome, my dear young lady, and excuse me that I do not rise. Nasi, approach that *fauteuil*. *Bon*. Now sit down by me, my dear, and remove your hat. *Ouf!* what a heat!" The speaker was reclining on a fully-extended cane lounging-chair, fanning herself with an indolent, rythmic movement. She was a large woman of about forty years of age, and must have been handsome till she grew stout ; her massive proportions, that were evidently untrammelled by any corset, were exaggerated by the shapeless white cambric robe she wore, and masses of waving brown hair were hanging loosely by the side of her face, escaping from a thick twist coiled low down on her neck.

Alma Belmont's first impression of the lingering, liquid tones that had greeted her was almost effaced by this superabundant and untidy vision, but presently she spoke again, fixing on her visitor a pair of soft, sleepy brown eyes that matched the voice to perfection.

"*Chère petite*, what a ridiculous little hat is that you have there ! Your pretty fair face is all brown and burnt, and your poor nose—those terrible mosquitoes, how they have arranged you ! Nasi, fetch the eau de Cologne, and a soft *mouchoir*, and dab her face ; *doucement*, you know—but first, come and kiss your mother."

The tall lad came to her and leant over her chair, and his brown curls mingled with her luxuriant brown tresses. As he left the room, she half raised herself and turned to Alma, saying, "Ah ! no one can tell what a son that is ! I had so longed that my little child should be a daughter, for I had one son already ; but he is son and daughter both, *ce cher* Nasi !" The subject of her eulogy here appeared with the eau de Cologne, but did not attempt the dabbing process recommended by his mother, who sent him again out of the room on a fresh errand to see and report if the evening meal were ready. He returned presently with his father, a quiet, gentlemanly man of middle age, whose thoughtful face bore traces of disappointment or dissatisfaction with life generally, that showed themselves in the lines on his forehead, and in the querulous tones of a thin voice. Of the Irishman, nothing, no accent, no vivacity, nothing but the name. With a courteous allusion to the introduction of his friend, the Collector of Bristowe, he gave Alma his arm, while Athanase dragged his mother up from her reclining posture, and they went into an adjoining room, where a cloth was laid with cold meats, fruit, and salad, cakes, tea, and lemonade, and adorned with flowers. Alma's head was aching frightfully, ·and she did but scant justice to the appetising repast, though it offered a delightful contrast to the greasy, ill-served meals on board the steamer. The little party had been increased by the addition of a good-looking boy of twelve, who, with his head resting between his hands and his elbows on the table, had appeared on their entrance to be completely engrossed by a book he was reading.

"This is our scholar," said the father, with a glance of affectionate pride. "Our baby, too," interposed the mother, who seated herself between her boys, while Mr. Bingham and Alma completed the circle at the round table. The hospitable hostess expressed herself *au désespoir* that her guest could not eat. Mr. Bingham said little, but his inquiries about books, politics, society " at home," all showed a hankering after the old country. It was easy to see that the duties of his life were not congenial, however close and dear were the home ties of the family. Alma could not restrain a sympathetic feeling of pity for the man who had probably hoped for and anticipated a very different career, while at the same time, surrounded by this soft atmosphere of home, her pity for herself grew stronger, and she envied the lot of the happy wife and mother.

Rising from the table, Mr. Bingham said he had " some work to do " ; the studious boy was going to " help his father with his accounts," and the two ladies and Athanase adjourned to chairs on the verandah.

" Ah ! but they are clever, my husband and Sosthène," said the Creole lady, "and Nasi here is my dear, good boy, and my eldest son, Hilarion, who is away, is *beau comme Apollon*." And so she babbled on with her simple talk, little knowing that she was planting daggers of regret in the heart of the girl who had cut herself off from home, and so keenly realised that she had bartered her birthright for a mess of pottage as bitter to the taste as the apples of the Dead Sea. When she had been further informed that Athanase was named after his grandfather, and Sosthène after his uncle, who were planters in the Isle of France, and that the good lady's own name was Zéphyrine, an incongruity upon which she herself commented with fat chuckles of enjoyment, Alma at last ventured to say that she was tired, and would fain retire for the night.

"Ah! my poor child! That I should not have thought of it! And you are pale—pale as this linen," waving a handkerchief that in the morning had probably been whiter. "Come; Nasi and I will show you to your room. Unfortunately, we have no spare apartment in the house, and it is really in the Custom House; but the bed is comfortable. You are young and tired and will sleep soundly, and in the morning early I will send round some one to you with a cup of tea. Come, *chère enfant*."

They proceeded round the verandah to the other side of the house and through the long, covered passage in the garden that they had skirted on Alma's arrival, then down a short one in the Custom House, into which doors opened from various rooms.

Under the closed door of one of them shone a brighter light than the dim oil wicks with which the building was scantily lit.

"That is where they are 'working,'" said Mrs. Bingham; "we will not disturb them—you are so fatigued, and I will wish them *bonne nuit* for you."

She threw open a door as she spoke, and ushered her guest into a large, cool, bare room, with two windows, situated at right angles to each other, one of which was shaded by a drawn down venetian, the other, which was long and narrow and barred with iron, had neither blind nor venetian, so that the bright moonlight streamed through it, illuminating that part of the room and leaving the rest in darkness. Lighting a little lamp that stood on a table near the bed, which, with a washstand, a couple of chairs, and a strip of Indian matting on the floor, constituted the whole furniture, Mrs. Bingham gave a motherly kiss to the girl, while Nasi clasped her hand in his lithe, lissom young fingers.

"*Bonne nuit! Dormez bien!*" and they departed. Left to herself, Alma's first act was to fasten the door and extinguish the little lamp, that was smelling vilely and aggravating her sick headache. Then she sat down on her bed, and tried not to think, but just to rest a little before undressing herself in the quiet, dark corner, swaying gently backwards and forwards with closed eyes, as if rocking her own lullaby.

At first, she could hear occasional faint snatches of talk, in which she recognised the voices of Mr. Bingham and his son, in an adjoining room. Presently, she ceased to distinguish them, becoming absorbed in the thoughts which crowded into her mind, whether she would or no.

How wretched she had felt on leaving Bristowe, and parting with the kind friends who had kept her with them after her husband's departure. Mr. Thornhill, fine, honourable English gentleman that he was—if a little proud, as some people seemed to think. Who, after all, had more cause to be so? And his clever, brilliant wife, who would have held her own as leader of a "salon" in the most select set of London or Paris society. The interesting daughter of the house, too; a little satirical, a little reserved perhaps, but so proud of her mother, and so singularly free herself from small feminine foibles and vanities. A charming family, whom Alma had learnt to love. Why were all her affections and friendships to be torn up almost as soon as they had struck root? These kind people, under whose roof she was at this moment, were hardly like strangers, but she would have to leave them, too, the next morning, and so probably it would always be.

Footsteps along a passage and the shutting of doors here interrupted the course of her reflections. Evidently Mr. Bingham and Sosthène were returning to the house. Then came a tremendous clang, as if a heavy door had suddenly swung to, and Alma could even fancy she heard a lock or a bolt shot. It must be the door of the long passage dividing the Customs from the dwelling-house. And all at once she realised that she was shut out for the whole night in a strange, empty, solitary building, quite alone !

It was not a pleasant feeling, for she had never been brave even as a girl, and had become a nervous, easily-agitated young woman. So she thought she would undress as quickly as possible and, child-like, bury herself and her fears under cover of the friendly bed-clothes. But her hand shook so that she could hardly manage to unfasten her dress, and the obstinate strings of a petticoat got knotted and entangled to such a degree that she was seriously contemplating jumping into bed without any further attempt at divesting herself of her ordinary attire.

Hark ! what is that ? A sound of footsteps outside the window—a kind of cat-like tread of unshod feet, and surely a dusky shadow goes past, and yet another and another ! Blacks ! Her heart, which had been thumping loudly, gave a great leap and then stood still. She had come across a few of them in Bristowe, town blacks, tame creatures, who spoke English and begged for pennies. She had only just begun to tolerate the young *gins*, with their little brown picaninnies slung over their shoulders, but the old hags with their pipes and their dilly bags, and the spindle-shanked men with their hungry, wolf-like dogs and their waddies, had always remained to her objects of horror. She never could understand why "King Billy," who wore a brass plate round his neck with the title duly set forth thereon, should be a *persona grata* at Riverview, where he was allowed the run of the offices, and quite failed to see what amusement the household could find in his mimic antics when he strutted about on the lawn. "Now, me Honourable William Thornhill. Wait; you see. Now, me Governor, Sir George." But, at any rate, he was partially civilised and harmless. All the blood-curdling stories she had ever heard or read about savage atrocities came into her mind. She shivered where she sat, and her teeth chattered with fright. What did it matter if the window was barred? Why, if they were only to look in, if she saw a black face at the pane, she knew she should die of fright. For a moment she contemplated snatching up a shawl, a towel, no matter what, and pinning it across the window: but that would only attract attention. Besides, she could not endure not knowing what they were about; at all risks, she must see for herself. So she got off her bed and crept along by the walls until she came to the window, crouching down so that her head was on a level with the sill.

The sight that met her eyes paralysed her with terror, so that, fearful as she was of being seen, she could not move from her constrained position. The bright moonlight made everything as plain as day, and the fires which the blacks had lighted around the circle within which they were congregated in some numbers threw up lurid flames, and cast fantastic reflections on the painted and besmeared faces of the warriors, who were flourishing their spears and nulla-nullas, and brandishing waddies above their heads in terrible mimicry of real warfare. Their hoarse cries and fierce yells mingled with the discordant music and monotonous chanting of the *gins*, who were beating tom-toms and swaying backwards and forwards as they sat in the background, with eyes fixed on the pantomime of their braves. The mimic combat was succeeded by a dance, if possible, even more terrible, in which the fighting men became so many grinning demons, with countenances distorted by every vile passion, dancing through the flames and throwing up their arms with wild screams and sudden shouts of fiendish laughter, such as one could imagine proceeding from the devils torturing the damned in the accursed orgies of an Inferno. Alma could have screamed herself, but her dry throat was voiceless. Her temples throbbed violently, and all the blood in her benumbed body seemed to have concentrated itself in her head, which felt as if it would burst. She turned sick and faint, and suddenly losing consciousness, sank down in a heap on the floor beneath the window.

How long she had lain there she never knew, but when she revived all was silent. Shuddering, while she nerved herself for the effort, she once more raised herself to her knees and cast a fearful glance in the direction of the scene that had been enacted. No traces remained beyond the ashes of the extinguished fires, strewing the ground where they had been lit. But for that, all might have been a hideous dream born of her frightened fancies and fevered imagination. Her trembling limbs could hardly drag her to the bedside ; but, reassured in a degree, though still quivering in every nerve, she was at last able to close her strained and aching eyes in a sleep of utter prostration and exhaustion.

Alma Belmont was young and strong in those days, however, and when she was awakened by the brilliant sunlight streaming into the room, followed by the arrival of the promised cup of tea, she was able to dress and appear at the breakfast table with very little trace of any more trying experience than the fatigue and indisposition of the previous evening. She had made up her mind to say nothing about it, being rather ashamed of her fright, for a little calm reflection had convinced her that her kind host would not have left her in a position in which she could have incurred any actual danger, that the ship was not far off along the quay, and that her alarm had been utterly groundless. She felt glad to have come to this decision when Mr. Bingham said he " hoped she had not been disturbed during the night by the antics of his black friends," that they generally chose a night when the moon was at the full for the indulgence of their pantomimic diversions, and that he had given them leave to assemble when they pleased on the piece of waste ground adjoining the Customs enclosure. He was sorry he had not warned her, as she might have been alarmed by a sight that must be novel and unexpected to a " new chum." To which Alma merely replied, with a smile, that his hospitality was quite on an Eastern scale in providing such entertainments for his guests, and that she certainly had to thank him for a new sensation.

But time and tide brought round the moment of departure. With a sob in her throat Alma bade farewell to the warm-hearted Creole lady, whose soft brown eyes rested on her through tears as she affectionately embraced her, and wished her *bon voyage!* She had not been allowed to refuse the offer of Nasi's last new straw hat in lieu of the *petit chapeau ridicule* that had aroused Mrs. Bingham's womanly concern for her " poor nose " and complexion ; and thus equipped, and laden with fruit and flowers in a basket, and other trifles that might conduce to her comfort and recreation, she watched the little party from the deck of the steamer until a bend in the river hid them and the township of Ellenborough from eyes that were dimmed by grateful tears.

She never saw any of the family again, with the exception of the absent Hilarion, whose acquaintance she made about a year later.

But that, as Mr. Kipling says, is another story.

II

AN HOUR IN TWO LIVES

THE pair on board the river steamer bound from a Northern township in Queensland to its capital were about the same age as far as years counted, and these might have been five-and-twenty. The young man had " lived," to use his own expression. The woman had had five years' experience of marriage—an unhappy one. She had been sobered and saddened by it, and in consequence, imagined that she felt very much older than she did, and mentally characterised her companion as "a remarkably good-looking boy."

The first time she saw him she had said to herself that there was too much of the Greek god about him, and " very little room for brains in that small head "; but her indifferent glance had lingered a moment on the classic contour of a face and form that excited a warmer admiration in most women than their antique prototypes of Antinous or Apollo.

On his side he had noted this initial indifference, and a dominant expression of sadness on a naturally mobile countenance. But he had also seen that the gaze o the dreamy, grey eyes could quicken to animation, ana that they lighted up even when the mouth sometimes remained set and serious.

He had heard about her from his own people, and others—of the unhappiness of her married life, and how it had been said at head-quarters that her husband would have lost his billet over and over, but for " that little wife of his, you know." He had long wished to meet her, and chance had brought them together a couple of days ago.

They had at once taken up a position of frank friendliness towards each other, and he had talked a good deal of his aspirations and ambitions, to which she had responded with apparent sympathetic interest. Still, he did not feel sure of the kind of impression he had made, or if when they met in the society of the capital, the *entrée* to her house would be allowed him for any other reason than that of previous acquaintance with his family. In fact, he had not quite made up his mind—in spite of what he considered an extensive knowledge of women—in what category to place her.

At the moment he wanted her to go on shore with him, but did not feel at all sure of her consent, or of his own powers of persuasion should she refuse. It would be pleasant to have a ramble in the moonlight while the wretched little boat was coaling and dropping cargo and passengers; but he was hardly surprised that she demurred to the proposition when made.

"I assure you, Mrs. Belmont, it would be quite impossible for you to remain on board while they are coaling. You have no conception how it would annoy you, and the captain says he will be quite a couple of hours about it. What would you do?"

"Well, I thought I would go to bed, you know, it's nearly ten o'clock, isn't it?"

"But you couldn't possibly go to sleep with the noise, and even if you half stifled yourself shutting down the port and drawing the curtain across your door, it wouldn't keep out the coal dust."

"So bad as that, really?"

"Oh! ever so much worse! Heat intolerable, men swearing, pandemonium itself! Do be persuaded for your own sake — everybody does. It can't be helped that you happen to be the only lady on board. I'll take such good care of you, and you cannot surely resist that moon."

Mrs. Belmont hesitated. She had not been long in this semi-tropical country, she knew people did things "out there" they would not do "at home," still, it did seem an *outré* proceeding to wander off till midnight in a strange place with a young man she had only known a couple of days on board ship. True, she knew his family, but this Hilarion Bingham had the reputation of being what was called "fortunate" in his relations with her sex, and it was notorious that her husband left her very much to her own devices—all the more reason that she should be more circumspect than a better guarded woman.

It would of course be very pleasant to leave the dirty, evil-smelling vessel for a couple of hours, and breathe a purer atmosphere in that glorious moonlight and the radiance of the Southern Cross—if only people wouldn't say ill-natured things and make her position more difficult. Life was bad enough while they spoke well of her; what might it not be should they speak ill or even think it!

Some of these reflections must have made themselves visible on her countenance, for even as she turned to speak, the young man arrested her unspoken words—" Don't vex your soul on the score of Mrs. Grundy," he said with a smile, "it would be nothing out of the way, and even if it were, there's nobody to say anything about it."

" There are reasons "—she began gravely.

" There always are," he interrupted. " We know all about that, Mrs. Belmont, and now that you have sacrificed on the altar of the conventions, and made your nice, proper little protest, you'll come, won't you ? "

Before she could utter the rejoinder that came to her lips, a young man crossed the deck towards them, calling out as he advanced—"You're going on shore of course, Bingham. I see the gangway is lowered, but it's rather awkward for a lady. You'd better let him go first, Mrs. Belmont, while I follow you, and between us, I don't think we'll let you slip over the side." The slight cloud that had contracted Mrs.

Belmont's pretty brows cleared off as she turned to the
new-comer.

"What an observant person you must be, Mr.
Young! So much more so than Mr. Bingham, for
example, who never noticed that I was frightened
out of my wits at the mere thought of venturing on
that ladder." She gave a kind of little shudder, and
continued: "Let us go before my courage fails me
again."

Hilarion Bingham turned upon her a look half
amused and half reproachful, and silently preceded
her down the rickety kind of ladder with one
narrow plank nailed lengthwise across the rungs
which had been thrown from the deck to the landing
stage.

"Easy to see they don't lay themselves out for lady
passengers," said the other young fellow, who was
following with both arms stretched out until his
hands rested lightly on either side of Mrs. Belmont's
waist.

"I had no business to come on a cargo boat, had
I?" she retorted with a little laugh, tripping over the
awkward bridge with the careless ease of a child, and
hardly availing herself of Bingham's outstretched hand
as she swung herself down on the quay.

Alma Belmont was not the sort of woman to put on
helplessness with an idea of making herself "interesting," and for all that Hilarion Bingham's beautiful
head was "too small for much brains," he knew this
much, and she knew that he knew it. The other
simple youth was much flattered by being credited
with superior powers of discrimination, and made a
remark to the effect that he had sisters, and ought to

know something about women, and that they always "liked a fellow to look after them, and that sort of thing, don't you think, Mrs. Belmont ?"

"We know that you want to look after *one* woman, at any rate," interposed Bingham, "and I am sure Mrs. Belmont will not wish to divert you from your allegiance, so don't hesitate about dropping our company at the corner."

The three had been walking abreast along a straggling kind of street, consisting of a few stores or shops with a one-storied dwelling-house here and there sandwiched in between them. They were for the most part dark and silent, as if the inmates were abed, but at the first turning—the "corner" alluded to—sounds of mirth and merriment and the music of a fiddle came towards them, proceeding from a brightly-lighted house, from which a signboard was swinging.

"Well, good-night, then," said Frank Young, stopping to shake hands with his friend. "They seem to be keeping it up still ; I expect the bridal pair, though, will have made themselves scarce by this time——"

"And pretty Lucy will want consoling for the loss of her twin sister, eh, Frank ? Good luck to your wooing, my boy !"

"Let me wish you good luck, too, said Alma, holding out her hand with a charming smile and gesture ; "I had no idea I was treading on the heels of a romance."

The young man laughed as he again shook hands warmly with the pair, and walked down the street with glowing eyes and rapid, elastic footstep.

"Now tell me all about it!" cried Mrs. Belmont, turning to her companion; "is it the innkeeper's pretty daughter, or who is responsible for that beatific expression on our young friend's ingenuous countenance?"

"Pretty sister, and a really nice girl, Mrs. Belmont. You have been long enough in the colony now not to be surprised if, indeed, I say a charming young lady. Report has it that the brother was an Oxford man; he is at any rate a gentleman, and a capable one to boot. He transformed a low public into a respectable house of entertainment, which has completely altered the character of the district, and when those twin orphan sisters of his came out to him instead of governessing for a livelihood, they found themselves treated like young princesses."

"And what of the bridegroom. Is the match a suitable one for this—young lady?"

Hilarion replied to the pause rather than to the question:

"Ah! I see you are incredulous. He is a very decent fellow, a surveyor, and there is plenty of work here for men of his profession. Young and he are starting together on a three months' expedition into the heart of the country the day after to-morrow, I believe."

"Poor young bride! A short honeymoon!"

"Yes, poor fellow! A short honeymoon indeed!"

There was a perceptible difference in the two intonations: a note of wistful regret in the woman's; in the man's a ring of impatience and some other feeling.

It was such a night as one sees only in the tropics,

flooded in moonlight and as bright as day. One could distinguish the different shades of leaf and flower, the delicate pink of the oleander, the greenish white of the seringa bloom, the waxen hue of the magnolia; the air was full of soft sounds and mysterious murmurs, laden with nutty fragrance and the heavier scent of the datura and trumpet-blossom. They had walked on till they had left the scarce habitations behind them, and Alma felt as if she were in some enchanted place. There was an unreality about this luxuriance of beauty, in the midst of which Hilarion and she were walking together as Adam and Eve in the Garden of Eden; its very loveliness oppressed her, and she gave an involuntary little sigh and stopped short. They had come to a kind of gully with a range of low hills on one side, on the slope of which was built a solitary wooden house, shut in by a hedge of prickly pear that surrounded it. It was new and unbeautiful, the trellised sides of the verandah as yet bare of creeper or vine, and the front open to the gully. By the roadside where they were standing lay a tree log, and a small clump of trees still further back cast a kind of shadow onwards.

"Let us stop here," said Alma; "we can sit down and speculate on that solitary, silent house, which would be almost ugly if it were not transfigured in this silvery radiance. And yet," she continued, "I would sooner make my home there than go on, go back to—" she stopped abruptly with a quiver of pain in her voice.

"Yes, I know, everybody knows," cried Hilarion; "go back to a man whose very presence is a degradation to your womanhood, to a life which must be one long endurance and martyrdom. "Why do you do it, you poor little woman? God, why do you do it?"

There was a note of passion in his voice that had not sounded till that moment.

"Stop, exclaimed Alma, "say no more; for pity's sake, stop, Mr. Bingham."

She shrank away a little, putting up her hand as if to hide her face, but he caught hold of her wrist and grasped it firmly while he went on with a torrent of rapid speech that she was powerless to check.

"You shall hear what people say about this husband of yours: that but for you he would not have a single friend or acquaintance, that no one would receive him into their houses. Do you know that you could divorce him to-morrow if you chose? What should hinder you from doing it, and entrusting your happiness to other keeping?" His voice softened as he spoke, and he dropped the hand he had grasped and laid his own gently upon it. "Don't sacrifice your whole life. He has himself disgraced the name he gave you. Cast it off, even if you accept no other."

Alma turned upon him almost fiercely. "Do you think I should take back my own, the name that I never sufficiently valued, the name that belongs to my brothers, who sustain its honour in the service of their country? You must have a very poor opinion of me, Mr. Bingham, for I fear, indeed, I have brought this upon myself. Let us go back to the ship." She spoke with dignity and made a movement to rise, but Hilarion gently restrained her, and her gaze followed his gesture as he pointed to the house on the hill-side.

"Look," he said, "look, we are in shadow and they cannot see us."

A lamp had been brought into a room opening on the verandah, where a man and woman were standing close together, the moonlight full upon them. The man's arm was round his companion's shoulders, and one of hers, from which the loose sleeve of her white wrapper had fallen, was raised against the verandah post, her head resting on her hand; she was looking out into the night with a rapt expression, while his gaze rested on her face. For a few moments they stood thus like statues, marble-white in the moonlight, the pair below motionless as they. Suddenly they saw the man put his hand under the girl's rounded chin and turn her head towards him, when she flung both arms round his neck and was almost lifted off her feet as he clasped her to him in a close, long embrace.

In a transport of passion Hilarion caught Alma to his heart with wild kisses that she hardly repulsed. The spell of the night was upon her, and the happiness of the wedded lovers throbbed and thrilled in her breast as in his, knocking at her heart with a clamant persistence.

"You love me, Alma," he whispered; "look up and say you love me."

As Alma raised her head, she saw the verandah was deserted, the lights extinguished, and the house once more in silence and darkness. With a sudden revulsion of feeling, like the snapping of a string too tightly strained, she burst into tears and thrust

Hilarion from her with a cry—"How could you—how could you?"

The reproach in her voice stung him like a blow as she sank sobbing on the tree trunk from which they had risen, and he uttered no word of protest or appeal till she had grown calmer; then he said simply—

"Forgive me, Mrs. Belmont; I was wrong. You do not love me, but I—love you. Give me a little pity for my love."

"Pity! I have none to spare. I need it all for myself. You knew it. You cannot expect that I should either pity or forgive."

She spoke with the cruelty, the perverse injustice of a woman at war with herself and unable to resist inflicting her own suffering on another, jerking out her words like so many lashes; and thus Hilarion felt them as he stood before her with head bowed and eyes cast down.

In the curious mechanical way that we see objects with our bodily eyes while the absorbed mind looks inwards, he became conscious of watching what appeared to be a piece of stick lying in the dust at a little distance from Alma's feet, and all at once it seemed to have changed its position and to be moving or dragging itself along the ground, till it had almost reached the hem of her dress. In a sudden he had realised her danger. Without a word of warning he lifted Alma up in his arms, and carried her some yards before setting her down again on her feet. As he did so, she struck him full in the mouth with the back of her ringed hand.

"How dare you? How dare you?" she cried furiously.

He had already gone back to the spot where she had been sitting, and was striking with his stick at a wriggling, hissing reptile. Then for the first time she realised the danger from which he had saved her. She was trembling from hand to foot when he rejoined her.

"Thank God you are safe!" he exclaimed, with an indrawn gasp of relief.

"I owe you my life," she said simply, then suddenly cried out, "But you are hurt—what is it?"

His face was lividly white from emotion, and he was holding a handkerchief to his mouth; as he removed it to reply, she saw that his lower lip was cut and bleeding, and again cried out anxiously, "Oh! what is it?—what is it?"

"Curious!" he said, with a smile that she felt to be worse than any reproach—"curious how remorselessly women can break a man's heart, and yet be pitiful over a drop of blood! There is no harm done, Mrs. Belmont. I was yours, and you have marked me with your brand—that is all!"

"And you saved my life!" She broke into a passion of tears.

"This is my reward," he said, gently taking her hand in his and raising it to his lips. "I do not ask again for love nor pity—nor even for remembrance. If you think you owe me anything, give me your forgiveness. It is a compact, is it not? You shall forgive and forget, and I will forgive and — remember."

He dropped the hand he held and waited, but Alma uttered no word. Moved by an impulse that she did not attempt to resist, she placed both hands on his shoulders and, with a grave tenderness that was almost a blessing, kissed him on the forehead.

"Goodbye, Hilarion!"

They stood a moment facing each other, looking each into the other's eyes. Then Hilarion quietly drew Alma's arm within his own.

"We will go back to the ship," he said. And side by side—nearer rather than further from each other in spirit since that mutual farewell—they retraced their steps in silence.

III

AN INN OF STRANGE MEETINGS

It was drawing to the end of September, and the consequent close of the season at Beauplage. Still a fair sprinkling of subscribers were patronising the afternoon concert at the Casino, and a small group of English visitors sitting on the red velvet raised benches at the end of the room (a coign of 'vantage from whence to discern the entrances and exits of one's friends and acquaintances) had been loud in their applause of a pot pourri of national airs played by the local band of the Casino.

"Do clap them for once, Mrs. Belmont," said the girl of the party, which consisted, besides herself, of her brother and mother and the very pretty woman whom she was addressing. "That nice conductor is looking this way, and it's his own arrangement, you know."

"But I so abominate such hotch-potch productions,

my dear child ; there's only one thing worse than these jumbles of airs, and that's the single air with variations."

"Well, I don't like that myself, when it comes to practising time," returned the bright-looking young English girl ; "each variation always goes on getting more difficult than the other, and one never seems to have half enough fingers. At least, I don't"; and she laughed out like the merry school-girl that she had only just ceased to be.

"Joyce is so delighted with everything," chimed in the gentle, middle-aged mother. "This is her first visit to France, and I am afraid, when we go home, she will find Dulwich very dull indeed."

"Very dull, *which* it is," echoed the brother, with intention.

"Oh! please stop him, Mrs. Belmont; he means that for a pun, and when once he begins——"

But Alma Belmont was at that moment giving a little intimate nod of recognition to a big splendid figure of a blue-eyed Englishman who was standing in the doorway, stroking a pointed brown beard with an unconscious, habitual gesture.

"That's the fellow who arrived yesterday, and a fine chap too! I saw him for a few moments last night in the smoke-room. Davenant, I think they called him. But he's an old acquaintance of yours, I believe," he went on, turning to Alma and following her glance as the new-comer bowed to the group with a slight comprehensive salutation.

"A very old acquaintance, Mrs. Marshall, and it may interest you to know that he 'stroked' the Brasenose eight over a dozen years ago, and could almost have stocked a silversmith's shop with his cups and racing prizes, for he was a runner as well as an oarsman."

"Didn't weigh fourteen stone then, I should think! But you don't mean to say he's *the* Davenant? Why, he left traditions behind him, and I know a lot of Brasenose fellows who would give their ears to have a yarn with him. Being a Brasenose man myself, naturally——"

"Hush, Guy! for goodness' sake don't get so excited!" interrupted Joyce Marshall. "That was the last piece, and he's coming our way."

"We may as well go down to meet him," suggested her mother, and presently they had all joined him and issued out together on the wide glass-covered stone entrance, and then through the gardens down the marble-paved port, Mrs. Marshall leading the way with her daughter, and Alma following with her double escort. When they had reached that windiest of all corners, known to the English colony as "Merriman's," Mr. Davenant paused and wished his companions good afternoon. He wanted to go in for a look at the English papers before dinner, he explained.

"See you in the smoke-room after dinner, I suppose," eagerly interpolated the young man, but Mr. Davenant was afraid not; he had promised to join a small whist party after dinner, at the Consul's.

"In fact," turning to Alma, "when the dear old man heard I was returning to London to-morrow, he wanted me to stay on to dinner, and I could not get off without promising at any rate to look in to-night. He had kept me at the Consulate the whole afternoon until I strolled down just in time to find you all leaving."

" Perhaps you don't know there's a dance on at the casino to-night," said Joyce—"the last one too. Couldn't you get away by eleven, Mr. Davenant ? "

" I shouldn't be any acquisition from a dancing point of view, Miss Marshall, having long given up such frivolities, and I hope to be getting some beauty sleep by that time," he concluded, raising his hat as he stood on the doorstep of the library with a look in his blue eyes that was half grave and half quizzical.

Later in the evening, when the guests at the big Hotel-Pension were mostly gathered in the drawing-room after dinner, taking their coffee before sallying out again, Alma Belmont was standing by a long French window half-opened to the balcony, listening attentively to a man who was leaning against it outside.

" Strange ! " Hugh Davenant was saying, " that after all these years we should both come back to the home of our childhood, the wretched little French town that we alternately abused and loved, and meet by chance in this caravanserai, then only to find you going about with a pack of uninteresting and common-place people, and I hardly able to speak half a dozen consecutive words with you ! The same old game ! Well, History does repeat itself with a vengeance ! "

" There are stranger things than that, Hugh ! "

" One of them being—— ? "

" That you should still care—— "

" Still ?—always ! Not that I was sure of it myself until I saw you again yesterday. And then it seemed only the day before that I had gone back to Oxford and heard of your marriage and departure for Australia, and all the old pain and grief came back again with a rush !"

"It seems a hundred years ago to me. Don't let us talk about it. Why in all these long years have you never married, Hugh ?"

"*Et tu brute!* " You can ask me *now*, now when at last I am in a position to speak, and you are once more free, Alma ! "

"If that is what you want to say, old friend, don't say it. My freedom is sweet to me, and I could never marry again ; I was too unhappy."

"But I would so surround you with loving care and devotion ; if you had only a spark of womanly pity or common gratitude.—Pah ! what drivel am I talking ? " He checked himself suddenly, and she interposed with a kind of strain in her sweet, clear voice.

"Had I any pity or gratitude in those old days, Hugh, when your devotion must have won recognition from any girl less ungrateful and selfish and heartless than myself ? I am no better now, rather a good deal worse, but I have thought sometimes that my unhappiness was a kind of retribution. You were so patient with me always, so kind and true, far more than I ever deserved."

"If you think so truly, Alma—and indeed I have always given you the whole love of my heart—you can more than repay me now. Only give me leave to take back my old place at your side as more than friend, more than brother, your unacknowledged lover still if you will it so, but not altogether as then, hoping against hope some day to obtain a dearer title ! "

He spoke in low, concentrated accents, which could have reached no other ears than those for which they were intended; and while the tardy reply was lingering on Alma's lips, a voice near them broke in upon the momentary silence.

"Are you not going to put on your things, dear Mrs. Belmont? Shall we wait, or go on and keep a seat for you?"

"Thank you, Mrs. Marshall, I am coming; I won't keep you ten minutes."

"Then you wil find us below in the courtyard." Alma turned back to the man on the balcony.

"Hugh, dear old Hugh, don't be vexed! I promise you shall have an answer in the morning. Give me a little time to think. Have patience with me!"

"I am not quite as long-suffering as I used to be, Alma," he replied with a touch of bitterness. "One gets tired of playing for ever the part of *l'un qui embrasse*, while *l'autre tend la joue*—and not even that, by Jove! Don't dare to play with me, Alma."

There was in his tone as much of menace as entreaty. Never in his life had Hugh Davenant so spoken to her; had he done so in "the old days" their lives might have been very different.

Now, like the woman that she was, her reply seemed almost inconsequent.

"Hugh! If you only knew how I have longed for a sight of your dear old face, for a grip of that great brown paw!" True affection looked out of her eyes into his own, and his hand held hers for a moment in a firm clasp.

Then she said in the clear, level tones that

characterised her utterance, "We both have our engagements to keep. Good-night."

"It will be for me a long night till the morning," he replied with gentleness; and not till he had watched her pass out with her friends through the big gates into the street did he leave the balcony that looked down into the courtyard.

Alma had told Hugh Davenant that the old days of which he spoke seemed to her as a hundred years ago, and as she sat in the brilliantly-lighted, mirror-panelled *salle* watching the dancers, all her youth passed in array before her mental vision. She saw herself once more a young, radiant, irresponsible creature, the centre of a throng of flatterers and admirers, grudgingly bestowing half a dance on one, unconcernedly sitting out half a dozen dances with another, either surrounded by Frenchmen, or discreetly left to a *tête-à-tête* with the favourite of the hour, and they were of all nationalities. Girls had envied, married women had been jealous of her, men had loved her to distraction ; she had gone on her way smiling, intoxicated with her own fascinations and triumphs, heedless of what might be said or thought; and what had been the outcome of it all ? Satiety, discontent, a reckless, unhappy marriage, exile, misery !

Absorbed in the past, her companion was unheeded until the return of Joyce Marshall with her partner recalled her to the present.

"Such a glorious waltz, dear Mrs. Belmont. How *can* you sit out ? Guy would be so awfully flattered if you would take a turn with him, and Mr. Hume was asking me if I thought you could possibly be induced,"

Both young men eagerly protested in unison that they would be "so delighted," "honoured," but Mrs. Belmont was not to be persuaded, and they went off to make up their set for the Lancers then forming.

Joyce was not going to take part in it, and Alma announced her intention of going up to the terrace while mother and daughter were together ; her head ached, the lights and dancers worried her, the sea air would do her good ; they were not to take any notice if she even did not return to the ball-room, as she might possibly after a time stroll back quietly by herself while it was still early.

In the general move of young people seeking or claiming partners, she slipped out of the *salle* quietly but not altogether unnoticed.

A man who had been watching her during the evening without attracting her attention, had followed her out of the ball-room and up the shallow polished staircase, then stepped into the empty reading-room for a moment when she had reached an angle at which she would otherwise have seen him. He had styled her in his mind a harmony in ivory and grey. She had kept on the white serge skirt she had worn in the afternoon, with the substitution of a creamy befrilled silk blouse for the jacket, and she carried a long grey cloak over her arm. Her skin was the same dead white as her dress, and her grey dark-lashed eyes were ringed underneath with amethystine shadows.

When she reached the covered terrace looking out to the sea, she drew a chair close up to the railing, and was sitting down, when her cloak caught on some projection as she attempted to draw it around her ; almost before she realised the obstacle it was deftly disengaged and placed round her shoulders, and a voice at her elbow caused her to turn round and face the intruder on her solitude.

"*Pardon*," he said with the languid drawl of a *petit maître*, "but this is not the first time by many that I have been fortunate enough to render you this trifling service, though not to Madame Belmont."

"Nor is it the first time either that I could have dispensed with the service, monsieur—in the past as now."

"Unkind as ever, the same provoking Alma! *Eh bien, tant mieux!*"

"Impertinent as ever, the same futile Fouligny! *Tant pis!*"

The little Vicomte threw his head back and contemplated Alma critically, as if he were appraising a picture.

"*Parole d'honneur!*" he broke out at last, "you have lost nothing, except—and I am not sure you are not the more charming—your roses!"

"And you—have gained nothing, except perhaps—" and she looked at him through narrowed eyelids—"a stomach!"

"*Méchante!* My contemporaries are almost all married men, and keep good cooks. *Que voulez vous?*"

"And why have you not 'ranged' yourself during these fourteen years and married also?"

"*A quoi bon?* My friends have mostly married pretty or charming wives (which was very kind of them), and I endeavour to show my appreciation, *hein?*"

Alma gave a little contemptuous shrug of the shoulders,

"You are an incorrigible, Monsieur de Fouligny!"

"Ah, madame, why not have married that poor de Bassompierre who adored you, and remained to us?"

"As one of the charming wives? I do not share your regrets, M. de Fouligny. But jesting apart and in sober truth, I should be glad if you would consider this little *entr'acte* over. I am tired. I came here to be quiet."

"I am mute, deaf, blind, whatever you would like me to be. I take this chair beside you and look in another direction till it suits you to recall me to life, then you permit me to escort you to your *domicile*. Is it not so?"

Alma made a movement of impatience.

"*Vous m'agacez enfin!* I need no escort; my friends are waiting for me below. I wish you good-night."

"Now indeed, madame, one realises that you have been amongst the savages. This is barbarity, but I obey."

Standing up, he drew his heels together in a low, ceremonious bow, and was turning away when Alma held out her hand with her charming smile and gesture.

"Not half the *mauvais sujet* that you try to make one believe, *mon cher*. Are you not tired of the old pose? Take my advice and study a new character."

"If you were here to coach me in the part, *qui sait? Enfin bonsoir, madame.*" And Gontran de Fouligny departed with a very creditable sigh, feeling for his cigarette-case as he turned in the direction of the smoking-room.

His inopportune appearance had disconcerted Mrs. Belmont, who had sought the solitude of the deserted terrace, not to bandy words in an encounter of wits with any frivolous Frenchman, but to dive down into her own heart and make up her mind as to what answer she should give Hugh Davenant in the morning. But the fact of once more conversing in the old familiar language had thrown her thoughts still further back into the past. She saw again the dark, grave face of the man who had been her girlish ideal, when, at eighteen—in love with Love itself, she had first met the man of thirty, who realised her every dream of what a hero of romance should be. The gallant soldier with an historic name, courted and beset by women of the world, to whose advances he opposed the shield of a calm indifference, had laid it down at the shrine of this innocent, girlish worship, but even he was powerless against the claims of *la famille*, that Juggernaut which can control the destinies and crush out the hearts of the sons as well as the daughters of France.

Alma loyally struggled against the flood of remembrance; she had risen from her seat and was leaning over the iron balustrade looking out to the moonlit expanse of water; the tide was high, and the swish of the waves against the seawall was distinctly audible. Suddenly, like the change of a slide in a magic-lantern, a fresh picture impressed itself upon her mental retina. In fancy, she was taken back to the shore of the great Australian tidal river where she had encountered Hilarion Bingham; they were together on the deck of the steamer, they were walking in the tropical moonlight of that enchanted Garden of Eden. His last words

rang in her ears—" Alma, soul of my soul, farewell !"
She cast a furtive glance around ; so vivid was the
impression that she almost expected to see the speaker.
Then a feeling of anger with herself took possession of
her, and she began to pace restlessly up and down
until the recurrent sound of her own footsteps begat
a fresh irritation. With an idea that any change
might dispel the obsession of her reminiscent thoughts,
she began to descend the polished steps of the staircase,
and almost unconsciously found herself out on the
marble pavements of the port before she realised that
she had left the casino. The quays were deserted,
even the cafés and restaurants seemed silent. She
began to think that the hour must be much later than
she had imagined, and instinctively drew the folds of
her long cloak closer around her as if to efface her
personality. She quickened her pace as a stray passer-
by cast a glance in her direction, then she fancied she
heard following footsteps, but went on her way reso-
lutely looking straight before her. At Merriman's
Corner a slight gust blew back the grey hood that
covered her dainty *coiffure* and slightly bared throat,
and as she was drawing it further over her head, the
flash of the diamonds on her ungloved hand suggested
a fresh cause for trepidation.

By the time she had reached the pension, her heart
was thumping in her breast, and her one thought was to
get in safe and unmolested. She had to pass the closed
gates of the courtyard and turn down the side street
in which her own quarters were located. When she
had first arrived at the pension earlier in the season,
it had been crowded, and a room had been assigned to
her in a house through which a communication had

been opened with the main building. Single people who did not care for large rooms, and those who merely required the night's lodging without board were generally housed in the smaller building ; but Alma had found her room comfortable, and had not cared to change it later. Now, as she fumbled nervously with her latch-key, she almost wished she had rung the porter's bell at the big gates, but while debating as to going back round the corner and doing so, the key suddenly turned in the lock, and closing the door quickly, she fled down the long passage, up the dimly-lighted staircase into her own room as she imagined. She did not know that in her fright and nervous agitation she had gone a flight beyond her own landing until, on rushing in and hastily closing the door behind her, she confronted a man who was rising from a writing-table, and recognised Hilarion Bingham.

Her trembling knees gave way beneath her, she sank helplessly into the nearest chair, and could only gaze at him without a word of explanation. His own surprise also at first arrested speech or movement on his part, but presently coming towards her, he laid a hand on her arm with a gentle touch that reassured instead of alarming her.

Speaking as if he had seen her but yesterday, " You have been frightened, Alma," he said kindly, as he quietly stood before her, "sit still and compose yourself, and then tell me if I can help you in any way."

His composure partly restored her own.

" I thought I was being followed out of doors," she answered. " I came in and rushed upstairs in such haste that I must have passed my own landing—my room is underneath. I must go down again."

Her breath still came in short gasps as she spoke, and she looked round with a scared expression.

"You had better wait," he said, "till I make sure there is no one about. I think every one is in except an Englisnman I met to-night at the British Consul's, my father's old friend, with whom I have been dining. He said he would smoke a cigar on the leads before turning in."

Even as he spoke, footsteps resounded and stopped at the end of a *corridor* running at right angles from Hilarion's; then they heard the closing of a door.

"Better wait a little longer. I will look out presently," he went on. "I am only passing through myself on my way to Paris, where I have left my wife," he continued, looking steadily at Alma as he spoke, "and shall be off early in the morning. Tell me something of yourself. How comes it you are travelling apparently alone and unprotected ?"

"I know every inch of the old place," replied Alma, with a slight note of protest in her voice, "and—I have been a widow for some years. You are happy, I trust, Hilarion. Do you still live at—— ?"

He answered almost before she had completed the question.

"Yes. I succeeded to my father's position when he died. Coralie is a niece of my mother's who came out to us from the Mauritius, and who is a dear daughter to her."

"I am glad," returned Alma simply. "Good-night, Hilarion." He looked out, and shut to the door for a moment as he took her hand in both his own. "Our little daughter is named Alma. You see I did not altogether forget. Goodbye ; *Dieu vous garde!*

Once again in her own room and the light turned up, Alma sat down at a table without removing her cloak, and began to write rapidly. At last she stopped to read what she had written :—

"DEAREST HUGH,—I married a man I did not love; I have loved two men whom I did not marry. The one love you know of—a sentiment, a romance bred in a young girl's imagination, heightened by obstacles, opposition. The other an infatuation that sprung up in a night out of circumstance, surroundings, the revolt of an unhappy woman !

"These books of my life are closed. If you care to inscribe your name on the third volume, I can still offer you a fair white page, and perhaps even a fresh heart. *Quien sabe?*

"ALMA."

She changed her walking shoes for slippers, still keeping on her grey cloak, with the hood drawn around her head and face; once more mounted to the second landing, passed the doors guarded by pairs of boots on each side of the *corridor* till she reached the one at the end and thrust the note underneath it.

When she opened her eyes the next morning, the smiling *femme de chambre* handed her a note with her early roll and coffee. "The big *Monsieur Anglais* of No. 20," she said, "had given her the *billet* for *madame. Bel homme, ma foi! et pas fainéant!* He was then going out for a walk before the *déjeûner.*"

Alma hardly waited for her to leave the room before

opening it. The envelope contained a man's visiting card on which a few words had been scribbled in pencil, and there was an interpolation that read thus :—

and Mrs.
MR. ⌃ HUGH DAVENANT.

University Club,
    Pall Mall.

"Come down ready to go out immediately after breakfast."

"At last I have found my master!" she said to herself, and sprang out of bed with a smile of exceeding contentment.

IN PEMBER BAY

PAPAITONGA LAKE

BY THE HON. W. P. REEVES

IN PEMBER BAY

PAPAITONGA LAKE

BY THE HON. W. P. REEVES

SAFE from the mountain tempest's wild alarms,
  Safe from the driving sea-wild's bitter spray ;
Placid, enfolded in the forest's arms
  Lies Pember Bay.

Did some known lover in his fancy's youth
  Name thee in accents musically slow,
Soft Papaitonga, " Beauty of the South "
  Called long ago ?

Midway between the mountains and the deep ;
  Secure from upland cold, from salt winds keen,
Bathed in sweet air and sunshine, thou dost keep
  A golden mean.

Dark clouds may brood on yonder peaks and spurs,
  Chill winds may chase the sea foam, flake on
    flake.
But here is peace.   Nought ruffles, nothing stirs the
    tranquil lake.

Nought shakes the ferns, whose interlacing fronds,
  Like sea-birds' wings uplift their giant pinions;
Nought stirs the brakes, whose creepers' myriad
      bonds
  Guard green dominions.

Look, while the sunset clings to yonder range.
  Look, while the lake gleams silver in its ray ;
And pray that though all beauty else may change,
  This scene may stay.

Here the wild birds from ancient coverts pressed,
  May seek asylum by this silent mere ;
And though no other glade or wave give rest,
  May find it here.

Though in an hour the forest fire ends all
  That nature can in patient ages build,
Though through the land the straight tall trees
      must fall,
  The birds be stilled,

Yet in this sacred wood no axe shall ring,
  These winding shores will sanctuary give,
Where in cool thickets happy birds may sing
  And verdure live.

Still for the singers be thy tree-girt edge
  And isle leaf-canopied a shrine secure,
Still for the swimmers be thy fringing sedge
  A refuge sure.

Long, Papaitonga, may thy ferns grow fair,
  Thy graceful toé-toé droop and sway,
And never tree or bird know scathe or scare
  By Pember Bay.

POINT DESPAIR

A MEMORY OF THE GREAT MASSACRE

BY H. B. MARRIOTT WATSON

POINT DESPAIR

A MEMORY OF THE GREAT MASSACRE

BY H. B. MARRIOTT WATSON

A GENERATION has slipped away since the Great Massacre, and even in this district in which I live, scarcely a hundred miles from the theatre of that abominable tragedy, the facts are almost forgotten, at least blurred to a fading _patch of colour. It is remarkable how swiftly time passes ; and what was yesterday a fear, to-morrow will become a reminiscence somewhat agreeable to talk over. Yet upon my mind are scored deeply the recollections of that horrible scene.

In the year of the Great Massacre I was in my eighth year, pretty sharp for a child, though somewhat undersized. My escape came about in this way. I had left Point Despair about eleven in the morning in the company of a lad, somewhat over my own age, who was returning to his people at Murimuru, some twelve miles distant. The road was plain and easy, running for some miles along the coast ; moreover, living alone with my uncle, I maintained a certain licence in my expeditions. Consequently I asked no leave to slip forth and accompany this playmate a certain part of his journey. It was a bright, warm day ; we had some sandwiches in our pockets, and there was the sea smiling with a thousand lures at our feet. The suggestion was irresistible ; we stripped to the skin, half way to Murimuru, and idled most of the afternoon in the water. It was not until my companion was suddenly pricked by his tardy conscience, and marched off, declaring he must make Murimuru with all speed, that I turned to retrace my way to Point Despair. The road, as it reached the point, dipped into a sparse piece of bush, through which it twisted irregularly for a mile or more, and ere I had issued from its shadows the dusk had fallen.

It was not at once that I was struck by the singular quiet which ruled the flat, for I was occupied at the moment with lively fears about my length of absence ; but half way to the post-house some uneasy appreciation of the stillness brought me up, and almost simultaneously I noticed a column of thin smoke rising at the back of Willis's lean-to. With that the significance of the silence went out of my mind ; there was plainly a fire forward, a most unusual event in our small settlement ; and, my anxiety forgotten, I broke into a run, thrilling under the stimulus of a new sensation. I had barely passed the lean-to in the dull twilight when I stumbled and went sprawling over something in the pathway. The thing gave under me, shifting a little aslant, and I cannot tell you my sensations when I perceived it to be a dead body. The light was still sufficient to see by, and ere I withdrew with a pant of alarm and terror I recognised the face, which was now staring up at me, as that of

Willis himself. The spectacle was horrible. I carry it still in my memory, as vivid and as ghastly as on that evening thirty years back. God knows how barbarously the wretch had been done to death, or perhaps the innumerable and dreadful wounds had been inflicted after the release of that poor spirit. My mouth fell open, and my eyes watched the dead man's fearfully, drawn with a nameless attraction. It was the first time I had ever encountered death, and I had no power of motion in my limbs. My legs shook, I stood transfixed ; the stare of those dead eyes held and terrified me. But presently the tide of reflection returned ; I took my gaze from the corpse and let it go round the vicinity. I was alive now, on wires of fear, ready to jump off at an instant's sound. But no noise came save the low, persistent murmur of the sea upon the shingle. Even then I had not conceived the fate which had fallen on the settlement. The horror had been so extreme that it had dulled my nerves, but as the blood flowed anew from my heart a certain reaction set in, and I was able to gather my wits together. I supposed that this Willis, who had never been popular with me for a sourness of temper, had met with an abominable accident, ?   ᵀ was the first to come upon the tragedy
shocking as it was in all the horrid circumstances of its presentment, roused in me an alacrity, and I hurried to be off. I turned from the still and stupid body, which as it lay had somehow a look of obscene importance, and I scuttled towards my home with all speed.

As I did so the dark and moving shadows of the column of smoke saluted my eyes once more. Vague and distant in my mind was a restless wonder of this appearance. I had a momentary presage of a wider fear, unintelligible but colossal, and then I was running for life with the terror of that defiled body at my heels.

The house in which I kept my uncle company was little more than a shanty, and lay about the middle of the four-and-twenty houses which constituted the township of Point Despair. The settlement held no street; it had not reached the dignity of order, and few of the plots were enclosed. A kitchen-garden, containing a handful of gooseberry-bushes, a few currant-bushes, and rows on rows of cabbages and potatoes, for the most part surrounded each dwelling-place. Macfarlane's house alone had the luxury of a verandah, and was, in addition, fenced with posts and rails, against which grew a hedge of *pinus insignis*. Here it was that I stopped for the third time. For the front door, flung wide, was squeaking in the breeze, and a figure in a woman's dress lay in a heap on the verandah.

The sight sunk me back into my abject fears. I would have fled past it on the feet of panic, had not a horrible fascination mingled with my terror. I had come direct from one corpse upon another. The bare fact of this sequence appalled and benumbed me, and yet once more I was drawn insensibly to inspect this second horror.

It was not so dark but I could make out every particular of that mangled heap. I remember that I pored over it stupidly, noting every ghastly detail, but comprehending little. My imagination suffered under a surfeit of the earlier horrors, and could digest no more. She lay with an arm clutching at her side ; it may be she kept some secret in that final moment, or perhaps it was merely by an instinct of defence. I could peer at the body so, but I should have shrieked out to have touched it with a finger-tip. When I left the verandah I had no proper sensations and no settled thoughts save a desire to get home. So incapable was I of further impressions that the body of a child in the pathway conveyed no meaning to me, though I was conscious that its name had been Sally. I merely accepted it as a natural part of this strange and rather terrible condition. I stepped over the child, backed away from it cautiously, keeping my eyes upon it, and then swiftly resumed my former gait. It might perhaps have leaped upon me. I knew not what would happen.

The smoke was rising from the ruins of the store, which stood only a few paces from my uncle's cottage. The flames had not worked much harm, as the fire had been unskilfully kindled, for the roof alone had been consumed, and the walls were still solid, but smouldering. Even the windows, though they were broken, showed still a few packages of grocery. The sight of the store, filled, as I pictured it, with innumerable sweets and treasures, struck me with more interest than the dead bodies, and for a moment I awoke to a thrill of excitement. But it was only mechanical, and I hardly paused to wonder as I dashed through the patch of cabbages to the door of my home. I had no thought of finding my uncle also dead, but the image of the woman returned persistently, and I glanced involuntarily about to see if perchance the body lay here also. As I entered by the door, which stood open, and my feet resounded familiarly upon the wooden flooring, something of comfort warmed me suddenly, and yet something of trouble too. I went clattering through the rooms, calling upon my uncle, a quaver in my tones.

The sound of my voice, solitary in the dusk, alarmed me further. No uncle answered me : there was no reassurance from the falling night. Indeed, the only noise that reached me came from the shore a mile away, where the waves of the Pacific moaned by day and night perpetually. It inspired me now with fresh terror to hear this melancholy sound, of which as a rule I passed unconscious, save on nights of storm. Inside the house it was more obscure than in the open road, but in two rooms I could swear that there was no sign of my uncle. One corner of the third was wrapped in deeper darkness, and upon this I stared with dilating eyes. I dared not enter and inquire there. Somehow the conviction grew in me firmly that there sat my uncle in the evil blackness of that corner with a grin upon his face, and on his body all the gross marks of those dead creatures I had seen.

I had ceased calling, and the silence frightened me even more than my lonely voice. Terror crept over me, at first gently, and then with a rush. It held my face blanched and fixed towards the darkness, lest something should spring from it upon me. The rickety table by which I stood shook under my trembling hands, and the harsh grating and creaking completed my horror. I yelled like a cat, and like a cat fleeing from the room dashed out of the house, down the garden and into the road.

I ran on heedless of my direction until my wind

was spent, and then, the original impulse of fear being lost in breathless fatigue, I stopped, and found that I was on the sandhills that filled the mile between the sea and the houses of the Point. The air was warm, and I was now all a-sweat from my running. I could hear the water roaring louder than before upon the beach. Inwards, where the bush lay black, in the rear of the houses, was a dreadful quiet. Somewhere across the dunes a *weka* called and was silent. The moon came out and shone faintly, for the night had already fallen as it is used to fall suddenly from southern skies. I was alive in a graveyard.

It was some time ere I was able to drag myself back to the houses. Indeed, I think nothing short of a new terror would have made me return. As I lay crouching in the "scrub" of the dunes my ears and eyes were preternaturally alert. The sand was covered with thin, rough tussock-grass, which shook and sighed in the wind. These sounds again discomfited me, and more particularly as the wind grew. A first breath of trouble, as it seemed to me, stirred through the long culms and set them gently whispering, as it had been the lamentation of a little child. Then with a slowly growing volume of wailing the reeds rocked and swayed in anguish, and it was as if the groans of that whole company of dead were expressed in my ears. The horrible tragedy, as I now conceived it, was enacted before me in these noises. As the wind rose I heard the shrieks of the poor women barbarously handled, and the screams and prayers of the dying returned to me ; and as it fell so I conceived again a silence to fall upon the settlement, which was the final stillness of death.

This impression made such a mark upon me that the beats of my heart quickened to a galop, and I began to see life start from the inanimate bushes and creepers about me. What nameless things I imagined were haunting those trembling and invisible bushes I have now no notion, nor indeed had I at the time. The dunes were alive with crying ghosts, and I was alone with them. I was stung once more into action, and with despair in my heart I crept from the open seaward space into the settlement again.

I took up my post now as distant from the houses as I could manage to be, without being actually beyond the precincts of the township. A space, still unoccupied, and the common playground of children, spread out before the store, and upon a slope in this, where the ground rolled up against a patch of bush, I sat in a heap of furze and watched the night. Some sparks of fire lingered in the beams of the store, and broke out into flame from time to time, revealing thick clouds of smoke that still rolled upwards to the moon. I took a certain comfort in this companion-ship, and after a time my terrors had so nearly subsided that I began to feel hungry; for I had eaten no food since midday. Though my spirit was returning, and my fancies were gone, I still lacked the courage to approach my uncle's cottage, or even to explore the store, in which I was sure to find some food. I endured the pangs with fortitude rather than face the unknown terrors across the threshold. But presently I remembered the wild fuchsia-tree which grew in the bush at my back, and with some of the *kanini* berries I stayed my appetite. The scene was so peaceful, and my refuge among the ferns was so warm that I grew even cheerful, and was soon whistling softly to myself; and when at last my extreme thirst compelled me to make a journey to the creek, two hundred yards away, I set out upon the expedition with scarcely any reluctance.

A house with a garden which in our wilderness had always been held quite magnificent, stood upon the verge of the creek. I had made the distance swiftly and in a respectful silence, but having taken my drink without accident I resumed something of my normal ease and security, and strolled back more leisurely, whistling the catch of a song. But at the gate of the house I was brought suddenly to a halt, my heart stood for a moment still, and I was rooted to the earth with the fear of what I saw. Something was moving under the white light in the rude track before the gate, crawling and crawling, as it seemed, towards me. It was not until the clouds streamed from the moon and the light grew clearer that I realised the cause of my stupefaction. It was the body of a woman, stirring feebly, and as soon as I had perceived this my fright left me and I drew closer and looked down upon it. I recognised her at once as Mrs. Stainton, a young woman of comely appearance, who since her advent to Point Despair three months before, with her newly-married husband, had shown me much kindness. She was still alive, and as I stood over her, not knowing what to do, she groaned and opened her eyes upon me. She lifted her hand and beckoned to me feebly; but I was reluctant to approach, and eyed her from a yard or two away. I saw her part her lips and struggle for speech. Her body writhed, and her features were contorted with her efforts. Her uplifted arm shook and fell.

But still I held aloof. In truth, I feared to approach lest she should take hold of me. She made a little upward motion of her head three times, as though she were striving to rise upon her elbow; but if it were so, the attempt was vain; her body quivered and her head sank back, and with a tiny sigh she was still. I waited a moment and then bent over her.

"Mrs. Stainton!" I called, "Mrs. Stainton!"

She returned no sign, and with alarm I perceived that her eyes were still open and were staring at me. I got up and ran away from the spot hastily.

Once in my lair among the bracken I felt safe and comfortable. The repugnance of the dead bodies did not pursue me thither. I was covered up from the eye of heaven in the long ferns, and in my warm seclusion sheltered from the wind by the patch of bush at my back. I soon began to nod. The walk of the afternoon had tired me and the mental disturbance of the last two hours had added to my weariness. I do not think I should have attached any importance to the very presence of the murderers at their work, if the tragedy had been re-enacted before me. Curled up, with my knees to my chin, I passed gently to sleep.

I awoke some hours later with a dismal squalling in my ears. I sat up with a start in that sudden panic that seizes on the dreamer while yet he is half-way to his senses. My heart thumped and my eyes strained through the cloud of darkness. Presently I recognised the sound as the mewling of a cat hard by. It came from the pines behind me, and drew gradually nearer; so that in a little while it had approached quite close to my refuge, where it stood, as I could see now in the twilight of the dawn, crying desolately. I jumped to my feet and put out my hand.

"Puss! Puss!" I called softly.

The cat darted away, limping on three legs, and I heard the sound of something trailing through the grass. I followed still calling on it.

"Puss! Puss! Poor Puss!" I said in a condoling whisper. It stopped forlornly before a heavy log of wood which barred its way, and threw a scared glance at me. I made a little rush forward, but the creature spat passionately at me, and gathering itself together, with an angry growl scrambled up the log, dragging a broken leg. It vanished with a screech of pain into the undergrowth.

I groped my way back towards the bracken disconsolately. My nest was difficult to discover, for I was still drowsy, and I wandered for some minutes ere I lighted upon it. I had scarce found the bush by which it was marked when my foot stumbled upon something, and being very stiff and sore from my hard bed, I fell forward rather heavily. I put out my hands to save myself, and they touched the cold flesh of a dead body. I screamed and fled blindly, escaping into my hiding-place, where I lay trembling. Those terrible things had followed me even there; there was no escape for me. I listened for the footsteps. Would it approach? The chill of something worse than death struck to my heart as I heard a slight movement in the grasses beyond the bush. I would have torn open the earth with my hands to bury myself. I cried out, calling on my uncle, who lay dead somewhere himself. Then there came a swishing sound; a cracking followed; and then with a sibilation of the tussock the Thing slipped out of the detaining grasses, and rolling with a soft thud from spot to spot, went down the little slope. I heard it pause in the hollow below, and silence once again prevailed.

    .   .   .   .   .

The sun was far gone in the sky when I awoke with the noise of horse-hoofs clattering in my ears. From the rise I could command a view of the road from the point where it ran into the bush ; and along this a horseman was cantering leisurely towards me. Save for the wounded cat and the last few moments of that flickering spirit the night before, this was the first live thing I had set eyes upon since my return ; and, once assured that it was no marauding Maori returning to his terrible work, I jumped to my feet, and scampered to meet the rider. The body in the hollow caused me a little gasp of fright as I passed it, all but treading on it again in the long grass. But even this reminder of my fears availed nothing against my sudden burst of joy. I ran down the road and met the horseman ere he turned the corner by the first cottage.

"Mr. Stainton ! Mr. Stainton ! " I called in excitement.

He threw a nod at me, but did not draw rein.

"That you, Johnny ?" he said. "What brings you up early like this ? "

Even as he spoke and passed by, without waiting for an answer, a nameless and delicate fear came over me. I saw him now heading his horse for that house ; and outside that house I saw what was waiting for him, beckoning me again with crooked fingers. For a moment I stood paralysed behind him, and then, a deeper instinct moving in my boyish mind, I ran at the heels of his horse, shouting in a treble :

"Mr. Stainton !   Mr. Stainton ! "

He must not, I felt dimly, be suffered to come wholly unprepared upon the remains of that tragedy. But my cries were ineffectual ; he waved his riding-whip as in greeting, without looking back, and cantered on. I stood for a space of time, not knowing what to do, whether to go forward or to retreat. Then, broken by my doubts and the dreadful thing my instinct scented, I took the latter course, and hid in the bushes again. It must have been a quarter of an hour later that I perceived Mr. Stainton coming back from the creek. He was riding fast, and his horse shied before the house with the verandah at something in the path. When he came abreast of me I rushed out, calling to him again :

"Mr. Stainton !   Mr. Stainton ! "

He turned his face towards me, and I saw that it was stricken ghastly white. His fingers shook on his bridle, and he stared at me, paying me no heed.

"Mr. Stainton, take me with you," I moaned. "Take me with you."

It was as if he saw me not. He went by like a flash, unheeding, with his grey face evil with terror ; and down the road I ran, sobbing and crying after him, till he had vanished into the bush and I was all alone again.

Yet this desperate and unavailing act had accomplished one thing. I had passed in my flight the limit of the township, and was now beyond the graveyard. Recognising this at last, I dashed into the bush, and that lamentable flat became lost to my sight.

Cætera desunt.

STRUCK GOLD

A SKETCH

BY MARGARET THOMAS

STRUCK GOLD

A SKETCH

BY MARGARET THOMAS

YEARS ago, before the whistle of the steam-engine had been heard in the land, or the pellucid waters of the Yan Yean had been laid on to the dusty streets of Melbourne, and long before Burke and Wills had made that plucky dash across the mysterious continent which cost them both their lives, when crowded ships were landing their seething crowds of fortune-hunting immigrants on the magnetic shores of Victoria, three raw youths from Somersetshire also arrived in Hobson's Bay. Like all new chums in that now distant day, they had come to make their pile in those golden fields, for the fame of the recent discoveries at Ballarat and Bendigo had reached even the wilds of the West of England, and farmers and farm labourers were eager to throw aside the spade and plough of old England for the more money-making shovel and pick of distant Australia. And big piles *were* made in those times, made not by buying shares in great mines worked by machinery and governed by a board of well-paid directors sitting clothed in black- cloth in luxurious

London offices, but by hard work of muscle and sinew, by heavy labour, and sometimes even by privation and suffering, of men in rags, under the broad glare of the pitiless southern sun. It is a far cry now to those picturesque and romantic days, and the younger race of Australians, who are growing up patriotically and justly proud of their native land, read about them as they read about other matters of history—the signing of Magna Charta, for example, or the Indian Mutiny.

Of our three "Zomerzet" heroes, two differed in no respect from the ordinary clodhopper one still meets in the remote recesses of that agricultural county; in a word, they were pre-schoolboard youths, and were, in the language of the virtuous young man of the Adelphi dramas, "poor but honest." But the third came under another category. He possessed both genius for art and the love of it ; and in spite of want of opportunity, in face of many discouragements and difficulties, he had, even at his early age, made a name for himself in London as a sculptor, and that seal of refinement which ever marks the true artist was set upon his whole being. Unhappily, too great devotion to his beloved studies had demanded the usual penalty, and doctors had declared that if he did not exchange the cold and fog of London for a warmer and clearer atmosphere, he would be obliged in a month or so to say goodbye to his models and statues for ever.

So he proposed to his brothers that they should accompany him in search of fortune to the wonderful Eldorado of the south, with whose fame all the world was ringing ; he even spent the last of his savings to

pay for their passages. Arrived in Melbourne, they
"humped their swags," tramped to the diggings as the
fashion then was, happy if they got ever so short a lift
in a bullock-dray, and lost no time in pegging out a
claim at Poverty Reef.

Months passed; the brothers worked as hard as
diggers only know how, when a stroke of the pick may
perhaps suddenly reveal to them an enormous fortune.
Saving, however, the few small nuggets which they
exchanged at the only store in the camp for the bare
necessaries of life, no good luck came their way. Day
after day saw them at their heavy labour; night after
night saw them sitting weary and dispirited round the
fire outside their little tent. Their fate was not singular;
hundreds around them were in the same case. When
one more lucky than his mates came across a pocket of
nuggets, or an extra big bit of gold, he gave them or the
notes he received for them to the landlord of the log
hut dignified by the name of "hotel," where whisky was
sold for five-and-twenty shillings a bottle, and telling
mine host to "let him know when the money was
knocked down," proceeded to drink till that event
came to pass, which it generally did pretty speedily.
The lucky man also invariably shouted for every comer
who cared to drain nobblers with him, till the diggers
didn't know a cradle from a pick, and the stock-drivers
could scarcely touch a bullock with their twelve-feet
whips, much less cut a piece out of its ear, as they
could do in soberer moments. When sick and heavy-
headed he recovered consciousness after his long booze,
the digger went to work again—but never a sadder, if
never a wiser man.

It was a cloudless night—one of those nights so

frequent in that land without mist or fog, when the moonlight is so clear that every detail is revealed instead of hidden, as they are in northern lands, and colours may still be distinguished. The moon's rays glimmered on the sword-shaped leaves of the gigantic old gum-trees, so that one might almost fancy they were gemmed with dew; they slid along the strips of bark which hung like rags from the rugged stems, and rattled in the scorching sighs of a fiery wind, which had now blown for nine days at least. In the distance stretched the primeval forest — immense, solitary, silent — the huge trees growing bluer and bluer as they marched in long procession towards the dim horizon, where a line of long low hills broke the otherwise level outline of the earth.

The air was heavy with the scent of wattle-blossom, mingled unfortunately with strong reminiscences of sundry dead horses lying in the near gully which the dingoes had not yet had time to devour; strange wild flowers—the creeping blue sarsaparilla, the red desert pea; curious orchids and heaths grew in the short dry yellow grass, every colour distinct in the brilliant moonlight, while here and there a sombre she-oak cast a deeper spot of shadow on the ground than the more feathery wattles and young gums could attain to. The harsh shrieks of a few belated cockatoos and parrots might still be heard in the bush, as the night fell quick and sudden over the earth, palpitating with the still nearly intolerable heat.

The camp was almost silent, the deep sleep of some of the worn-out gold seekers undisturbed by the rude shouting and laughter which denoted the whereabouts of the drinking shanty.

Two of the brothers, Jack and Will, came wearily in from their labours—utterly down on their luck, knee-booted, red-shirted, sunburnt, and mud-stained. They now looked like old hands; and as they threw their implements on the ground with muttered curse at their ill-luck, few would have recognised in these bearded men the fair-faced country youths who stepped on shore at Williamstown barely more than a year ago.

One of them proceeded to strike a match on the leg of his corduroys, lighted a candle, and stuck it in an empty bottle; the air, stagnant and warm, did not even cause the flame to waver. A fire was then made, a billy-full of water put on to boil, and Jack, taking some flour from a scantily-provided sack, proceeded to make the traditional damper, and put it in the hot ashes under the pot to bake. A handful of tea was then thrown in the bubbling water, the liquid poured into pannikins, and having seasoned the draught with coarse brown sugar, the brothers began their evening meal. Their funds did not run to mutton, so they munched their damper alone, with the appetite which youth and labour always appear to command.

"Where is Ned to-night?" said Will, cutting a huge morsel from the smoking cake with his bowie knife.

"Oh, loafing round, I suppose. Trying to see if the clay hereabout is fit for making images," responded the other. "Never saw such a chap for Art as he is. He'll never make a digger."

"What's the use of digging?" returned Will. " Here we've been working for months like niggers, and we haven't even a bit of tinned meat to put in our mouths, let alone plum duff."

"Take my word for it ; we shall strike gold soon, and strike it rich," said Jack. "The pipe-clay looked uncommon like it to-day; but what with the heat, long hours, and starvation fare, I couldn't get on any further to-day."

"Luck's against us, mate," said the despondent Will.

At this moment in rushed Edward with a fragment of newspaper in his hand. Oblivious to the fact that he had eaten nothing since their early morning meal, he cried, " I've made up my mind to go down to Melbourne at once. See here, they are advertising in the *Argus* for a sculptor to do some work for the new Government buildings, and I mean to go and try for it."

"Don't be a fool, lad," said the two brothers at once. "Here we are almost within sight of the gold, and you are going to chuck away your chance for the sake of a beggarly statue or so !"

"I don't care about the money ! It's three years since I have touched a bit of modelling clay, or a block of marble, and I can't stand it any longer. Better starve at Art than live in luxury without it. I'm off by daylight to-morrow morning."

" You'll have to walk then. There's no shot in the locker to pay for Cobb's coach."

"Yes, I know. I can walk to Melbourne in a little over a week, and if I can get the job I will " ; so saying he set to work to finish the remains of the damper and the nearly black tea.

Sunrise next morning saw the artist on his way, and it may be added here that when he arrived in Melbourne he got the commission for and executed the work so dear to his soul. It was the commencement of a busy and not unsuccessful artistic career.

But sunset that evening saw his brothers in a state of frantic delight bordering on delirium. They had finally struck gold, struck it in apparently inexhaustible quantities ; lumps of the gleaming metal lay embedded in the teeming soil where mother Nature had carefully stored it up long centuries ago to supply the needs of her children in these latter days. As nugget after nugget gleamed in the pale light of the miner's lamp, a sense of greed and arrogance sprang up in the hearts of the young men, and when at night they staggered to their tent under the heavy and dangerous burden of their newly-acquired wealth, they sank to the ground overpowered, with scarcely strength or sense enough to bury it under their sleeping-places, yet determined it should be theirs, and theirs alone.

And the two brothers became rich men, rich among the richest men of a wealthy colony.

But the artist, who for the love of Art had left the claim before gold was struck, had no share in their prosperity, he reaped no reward for his long and arduous labour in it. But he had that reward which is greater than riches—success in the art he loved, a career full of honour and glory ; at his death his adopted country mourned him greatly, and a monument was erected to him in his native country, where his name is still held in reverence, as it would not have been had he merely "struck gold."

THE LARRIKIN OF DIAMOND CREEK

BY E. W. HORNUNG

THE LARRIKIN OF DIAMOND CREEK

BY E. W. HORNUNG

THE Reverend Charles Caradoc was tramping in
from Heidelberg : not the old-world German
city, but that pleasant Melbourne suburb which was
idyllic before it became a suburb at all. Then the line
was only talked about, and you had to walk home if
you missed the last 'bus. Caradoc had missed it with
his eyes open, and was revelling in the two hours'
penalty. Through the wintry starlight his face
beamed pink with good-humour and enthusiasm ; on
the hard, undulating road, his step was the tattoo of
health and strength, of infinite confidence and complete
youth.

Yet there were younger men, and even curates, as
there were thousands more prepossessing in appearance.
Caradoc was eight-and-twenty, and he wore a moustache, which is seldom in its place upon a barrister, a
jockey, a man-servant, or a clergyman. This moustache was reddish, and of the horse-shoe order, but not
heavy enough to hide the wearer's good, but rather
prominent, front teeth. Caradoc had also very good
blue eyes, but these again were a little prominent.

Altogether you will picture him no Apollo. He had, however, a deep chin, a man's mouth, and one of the kindliest, most ingenuous, least self-conscious expressions ever worn between a clerical collar and a soft felt hat.

But he was a very new chum, having come out with Archdeacon Huntley, who had been home to England for a few months' holiday after thirty years' ministry in the colony. Greedy for honest work, and impatient of what went by that name in his country curacy, Caradoc had fallen in with the Archdeacon at a garden party, had confessed his discontent, and been promised his heart's desire if he would come to Melbourne. He was getting it among the larrikins of Carlton and of Fitzroy; in the tide of riff-raff that flowed southward, with thickening scum, to the confines of Little Bourke Street itself.

So his head and his hands were full; so his heart and his step were light; and the quick music of his youth and energy had drummed through Ivanhoe and Alphington, and was ringing down the hill to Diamond Creek, when that happened which stopped it for the moment, and changed it for the night. Curiously enough, Caradoc was thinking of a story told him that afternoon by the driver of the omnibus, the story of a man shot dead by a notorious bushranger at this same Diamond Creek, when history flattered itself with a weak repetition : a weedy figure flew out from the shadows, and a revolver was presented at the curate's head.

"Bail up !" cried a nasal voice, hoarse with excitement.

Caradoc stepped back, marking the lethal barrel.

This was agreeably short, and the starlight scarcely shimmered in its rust ; moreover, it was not covering him.

"Bail up ?   What do you mean ? "

"Yer money or yer life !" came in the still older formula and a still thicker voice.

"My life," said Caradoc, calmly—"if you can hit me from where you stand."

"I will—*my* word ! "

"I don't think your barrel's long enough."

The muzzle was spinning in circles like a midge. The curate laughed as he stepped towards it.

"I'll come nearer.   Now try."

And he fixed his good blue eyes on the hungry brown ones of a pitiful stripling, seen more clearly every instant in the starlight, and every instant a more painful exhibition of insufficient effrontery and oozing courage.   The end was in keeping with the rest : instead of being fired, the pistol was flung at Caradoc's head, whizzed over it, and went off like a squib as it clattered in the road behind him.   When he rose from ducking, two bare feet flashing under the stars was all he could see of his assailant.   He gave chase in his well-soled boots, and for a time the music was very fast ; it rattled over the bridge across the creek, and up-hill indomitably on the other side ; but towards the top it stopped suddenly, then turned into a duet of gasps.

"Am I to hang on to you," panted the curate, " or do you give in ? "

"Oh, Lord ! I give yer best—I give yer best ! "

"Then we go back to Melbourne together.   I can either twist your arm behind your back and force you along——"

"Ow! ow!"

"Or we can go arm-in-arm as though we were old friends. You prefer that, eh? Then come on!"

They went on without a word. Gradually their hard breathing subsided, and the parson took out his handkerchief and mopped his face; the captive did much the same with the back of his sleeve, only it was his eyes that required most attention.

"Whimpering at the thought of gaol," mused Caradoc. "Let him whimper!"

On the outskirts of the city he hailed a cab, pushed his prisoner into it, and told the man where to drive in a voice inaudible within; not until they stopped at his lodgings in Carlton did he hear that nasal voice again.

"Where are you bringin' me?"

"Come out, and you'll see."

Caradoc's supper was laid in his room, for he had only gone to Heidelberg to deliver a letter of introduction, and had said positively that he would be back; but he had reckoned without his kind colonial host, and had fared sumptuously before leaving the farm. Yet he rubbed his hands at sight of the cold sliced mutton, the loaf and butter, the pickles and the cheese.

"Capital!" he cried. "I've had my supper, Mary, but here's a fellow who I fancy has not. It just fits in."

And Mary withdrew without comment; for this was not the first dilapidated visitor that the curate had introduced during his short tenancy; and he had given fair warning that there would be more.

"Now," continued Caradoc, "sit down and have at it!"

Instead of doing so, the lad stood trembling like a frightened colt; his dark eyes big, and his brown skin blanched, with a deeper and a keener fear than even this coward had displayed on the road.

"What are you givin' us?" he gasped, in yet another formula.

"Mutton and damper, I believe you call it," replied the curate, looking for his pipe.

"Ain't you goin' to gimme to the coppers?"

"That remains to be seen. Not till you've had something to eat, at all events. Matches gone, as usual; got one about you, by any chance?"

"No."

"Ah! I've found 'em. Mind if I smoke while you're eating?"

"*I* ain't agoin' to eat."

Caradoc took a single glance at the set and sullen face; then he struck a match, and answered as he lit his pipe, with his back turned.

"Don't be a young fool. (*Puff, puff.*) I know very well why you stuck me up to-night. (*Puff, puff, puf-f-f.*) Isn't that the expression? Or is it that only when you're a bushranger? If you're a bushranger (*puff*) I'm disappointed in 'em; but I should be sorry to think you were one, for their sake as well as yours. All I believe you are is a half-starved larrikin——"

"That's all, so help me!"

"Then there's your supper. Stow it away! But, look here, if you turn on the waterworks, I *will* send for the police—like a shot."

An hour later, the curate and the larrikin were seated at opposite sides of the fire. The curate was in his third pipe ; the larrikin would not smoke ; and though the pale brown face was almost serene in its physical satisfaction, the dark brown eyes reached ever furtively for the door.

Caradoc took his pipe from his teeth, catching the glance.

"Must you go back to Diamond Creek to-night ?"

"*My* word !"

"You could have that sofa if you'd stop."

The larrikin fidgeted, looked down in discomfort, looked up in blunt inquiry.

"But you was goin' to get me run in ?"

"Oh, no, I wasn't."

He must have known it ; he only sighed relief.

"Then you'll let me clear ? The old man'd give me hell if I didn't go home !"

Caradoc took no notice of the word.

"So there's an old man, and a home, too, eh ?"

"Not much of one," laughed the larrikin. "Plucky home !"

"Do you know that you haven't told me the old man's name, or yours ?"

"Wot's the good, when he has so many ?"

"But he must call you something," remarked the curate, smiling behind his red moustache.

"He calls me things wot'd make your hair curl !" replied the larrikin, and Caradoc showed those promi-nent white teeth of his as he laughed outright in his own despite. Next moment he was particularly grave : as shyness wore off on the other side, it was his habit to drop a certain familiarity which he had found indispensable for putting the Melbourne larrikin at his ease : so now he suddenly ceased smoking at two pipes and a half, and stood up stiffly on his hearth-rug, with his long coat tails to the fire.

"If you like it better," said he, rather loftily, "what am I to call you?"

"*I* don't see as you'll have much chance of callin' me anythink," replied the other, with a snigger.

"Very good. Then you certainly shan't clear out. *Now* what's your name?"

The reply was slow, sullen, and uncertain:

"Willyum."

"William, eh? Well, William, you shall clear out, as you call it, on certain hard-and-fast conditions which you'll break at your peril. Refuse them, and I give you in charge."

He felt it a mean threat, an ignoble coercion; but if any end could justify any means, surely it was the end which he had in view. Nevertheless, when William had accepted the inevitable, with a sudden desperation following upon a frank reluctance, and equally suggestive of sincerity, the master of the situation felt a genuine relief, and made haste to adopt a less terrible tone.

"Know Lygon Street, William?"

"*My* word!"

"Know St. Cuthbert's—half-way down?"

"Outside," said William, with a fine ungodliness.

"You shall know the inside, too, before I've done with you," the curate promised him. "But one thing at a time. There's a mission-room a little lower down on the same side—a red-brick affair. You've got to know the inside of that first: you're to let me see you there every Wednesday and Saturday evening, at eight o'clock, till further orders!"

William sighed.

"To-day's Tuesday," continued Caradoc ; "you begin to-morrow night ; and I don't think you'll hate it half as much as you think. The other fellows don't. Lots come—lots of greater villains than you. I shouldn't care to be stuck up by some of them, William—*they* wouldn't mean it for a joke!" he added, as the boy turned a warmer brown. "But they aren't such bad fellows either ; they come and play bagatelle and draughts and dominoes ; we let them smoke, but kick them out if they swea."

Caradoc was disappointed. He had hoped that the programme — the Wednesday and Saturday evening programme — the kindergarten class in elementary decency—would appeal to this larrikin in the mere prospect as it had done to others. He was mistaken. William did not brighten ; he had been brighter before. All he did was to sit and stare into the fire, crass and unattracted.

"I forgot," said Caradoc. "You don't smoke, and you won't swear. Perhaps you read ? "

" *My* word ! "

"Then you can read there to your heart's content. One end of the room's for nothing else ; magazines, books, papers, and no talking allowed."

The effect was magical : it brought William to his feet.

" I'll be there to-morrow night."

" You promise ? "

"My oath."

"Then that's a bargain ; your hand on it, William . . . . And now there's just one more thing I want to know, and you shall go. I want a plain answer to a plain question ; you mustn't be hurt. Supposing I'd given you my money on the road—it's the last time I'll speak of it—would the old man have got it, or would he not ? "

The look was enough ; it was a look of swift, open-eyed amazement at Caradoc's insight. He smiled and nodded, rather proud of it himself.

" I thought as much. So he sends you out to make money ? "

" Day an' night."

" That way ? "

" That's my look-out."

" He wouldn't know, eh ? "

" No, nor care ! "

"I see," said Caradoc, looking into the bright, brown eyes, and disliking their moisture in a lad who was almost a man. " I quite understand ; and there's nothing to take to heart so much as all that, my good boy. It wasn't your fault—I don't blame you a bit. But, I say, you'd better take some money back, hadn't you ? Look here, you shall see what you'd have got. . . . Three-and-seven, exactly—a noble haul ! Take it, my dear fellow, it'll be better than nothing ; and one of these days you shall earn it honestly and pay me back. We must put you in the way of earning some-thing, of course ; but you shall come in to-morrow night, and have another square meal to walk back on ; and we'll talk it over then—if you won't be such a baby ! "

And Caradoc stood impatiently on the landing while the bare feet stumbled downstairs and over the linoleum ; when the front door slammed, he returned to his room and refilled his pipe.

" If he wasn't such an infernal baby !" he muttered
as he struck the match.   Yet the baby grew on him
as he sat and smoked, and put up his feet on the empty
chair opposite.

The site had been bought, the room built, the
Mission started by Archdeacon Huntley's sons—fine,
hearty fellows who did almost as much good in
Melbourne as that dear divine himself.   It was the
young men who had gathered in the larrikins, and
the young men who had taught them to appreciate
their privileges by kicking them out again as often
as necessary.   At first the necessity had been almost
nightly ; the character of the place very nearly non-
religious, as it still was on Wednesdays and Saturdays ;
but gradually it had become possible to establish a
specific ideal, to accentuate this as time went on, until
the mission-room could afford to avow its allegiance to
the church hard by.   So the enterprise flourished, until
it grew beyond the surplus energies of mere laymen,
and Caradoc on landing found his work cut out for
him ; what was better, he might himself have been
cut out for the work.   Good-humoured and yet firm
—but his qualities need no bush.   Of the highest
order they were not ; but for dealing with the
Melbourne larrikin they proved a well-nigh perfect
combination.

And yet a certain innate bluffness, which stood
Caradoc in stead with the ruck, did not always serve
him with the individual ; certainly it did not answer
with the half-hearted desperado who had attempted
to stick him up on the Heidelberg road.   The lad
came regularly to the room, but Caradoc never knew

how long he would continue coming. He did not grow more manly on further acquaintance; yet the curate did not like him less. He was not popular with the other boys: he was shrinking and self-conscious in their midst; yet Caradoc liked him well enough to ask him sometimes to his rooms, to resent his invariable refusals, to lend him his own books instead, to set him on the way to Diamond Creek, to feed his mind as they walked. And he seldom laid himself out to feed the mere minds of the rest; all his time was taken up in purifying their hearts.

So the short winter ended, and the long summer began; but before the great heat a feast-day was fixed, and the date announced by Caradoc to his larrikins, amid astonishing enthusiasm; for some of them knew, though he did not, the kind of day that it would be.

Quite in the bush, down the Gippsland line, Archdeacon Huntley had a twenty-acre selection, and a wattle-and-dab hut to which he and his sons would repair, now for hard, solitary work, now for complete rest and change. It was only thirty miles by rail; then there was a drive; and in a couple of hours all told you were in the heart of the wilderness, amid huge boulders and forest ferns, and trees taller than any steeple in the southern hemisphere. Hither, once a summer, Archdeacon Huntley brought his choir-boys for the day; and here the larrikins had their separate outing, with the Archdeacon and all his available sons to keep them in order.

There was a sound repast on the grass behind the hut; there were games, competitions, tree-climbing, stick-whittling, an organised exploration of the wilds;

and before tea, a general and compulsory bathe in the big waterhole. The young fellows acted as whips, but their office was a sinecure : the difficulty was not to persuade the boys to go in, but to induce them to come out. Caradoc suggested a strict time - limit, and stood watch in hand on an adjacent boulder, christened the Tarpeian Rock by the classical Arch- deacon, who stood beside him smiling benignly upon the brown hands and faces and the white bodies of the boys, wet and flashing in the sun. But the curate did not smile ; he frowned ; and his frown was blackest when he closed his half-hunter with a vicious snap.

"There's one fellow cut it, after all ! "

"Indeed ! " said the Archdeacon. "Which boy is that ? "

"His name is William."

"William what ? "

"Nobody knows ; he refused me his surname when I first got hold of him, and I have never pressed him for it."

"So he is one of your boys ? " said the Archdeacon, kindly. "I hear there are so many of them already ! You are doing a very noble work, Caradoc ; it was a good day for us all when I fell in with you."

Neither the Archdeacon nor his sons knew under what circumstances Caradoc had fallen in with the missing larrikin.

"I fancy his father is a great villain," continued the curate, blushing at the praise. "The lad himself is all right, if only he were more of a sportsman. This is so characteristic of him ! Goodness knows where he is ! I am sorry," he added with less emphasis, and more to himself : " I have a soft corner for the fellow in spite of it."

Yes—in spite of the very faults he could least endure —it was a softer corner than the curate could understand. His own tolerance puzzled him. Another skulker he had lashed with his contempt; another muff he had tormented into manliness, long weeks before this. It was as though the very badness of this lad's beginning, the abortive highway robbery, had imbued the object of that outrage with a special lenience towards him, less paradoxical than it might appear, since anything short of crime must in him henceforth assume a merit.

Not that Carradoc argued thus : he was one of the least introspective of mortals. His subtlest feeling was a slight impatience with himself, a naïve wonder that his day should be so easily spoilt. Yet he never hesitated as to what he should do : when the boys were finally in the brake, and the cheering at its height, it was the curate who ran up last and hottest.

" May I have one word, Mr. Archdeacon ? I can't find that boy anywhere ! "

" God bless my soul ! "

"I fear something has happened to him ; or he's run away to avoid going back to town. But we can't allow that ; he must be found."

" He must, indeed," said the Archdeacon, looking at his watch ; " but we must also catch our train. There is no other to-night. I think the best thing will be for one of my sons——"

" If you will permit me, sir, I would much rather stay myself. I know this lad ; he has a peculiar disposition ; but I believe I can manage him. I should deem it such a kindness if you could spare me to find him and to bring him back."

So the brake waddled down the rough track, and Caradoc was left behind, waving back to the waving lads, and returning their cheers until the great trees swallowed them: then he ran back into the selection, and mounted the Tarpeian Rock which was its highest point.

The sun had long been among the trees, but then the trees were so tall. It might be light for the better part of another hour. Caradoc stood on the rock, the golden glare showing the day's dust upon his black clothes, the day's own coat of red upon his heated face: the prominent white teeth were parted, the prominent blue eyes filled with anxiety and distress. And as he stood, the sounds of the bush, drowned all day long by those of a city, broke upon him for the first time: the whisper of leaves and grasses, the chit-chat of parakeets, the guffaw of a laughing jackass, the chirrup of locusts invisible, innumerable. But of the sounds for which he listened—a timid hail, a swishing of the ferns, the breaking of a branch—not one fell upon his straining ear.

It was his very first day in the bush; but he had met old bushmen in Melbourne, had visited them in the parish, and got on terms by a genuine eagerness to hear of the wilderness and all its ways. Now something that he had heard came back to him; he was off the rock in an instant, and following the posts and rails that enclosed the Archdeacon's twenty acres. If the fugitive had crossed the fence, he should find the place, the trail; but he never did; nor was there need.

From a brake of ferns two glittering eyes drew his; the green fronds rustled as in a sudden wind; the hapless William was run to earth.

"Thank God!" gasped Caradoc, but with that cry his tone changed. "Come out of it, you young idiot! What the mischief do you mean?"

William showed his face—very brown and sullen, and his shoulders—round with shame. But the brake was breast-high, and he evinced no disposition to come out.

"Why did you do it?" cried the curate. "Are you so frightened of cold water?"

The dark head hung lower, and in the red-gold glare there was a sudden glitter of tears, that fell like great diamonds upon the greater emeralds of the sunlit ferns.

"Is there no manhood in you?" pursued Caradoc; but even as he spoke the scorn fell out of his voice, and the question, that had broken from him as a harsh taunt, died away a whispered question and nothing more.

The answer was a wild covering of the hot, brown face by the tremulous brown hands, a pitiful heaving of the high shoulders, and such a storm of sobbing as might have wrung the heart of a stone. Caradoc stared and listened as though stone all over. And the crimson killed the gold in the failing light; and it warmed the quivering fingers, and what of the wet face they failed to hide, to the hue of burnished copper.

"So you have deceived me all these months!"

He was kept so long waiting that he was forced to repeat the question. He repeated it in a sterner tone, of which he felt instantly ashamed; but even this only elicited a whisper, inaudible, incoherent.

"I can't hear," said Caradoc gently; "I'm sorry. I'll come nearer."

"It was all the old man," the girl's voice whispered. "He didn't care so long's I brought something home . . . there were worse ways . . . *he* didn't care!"

"You shall never go back to him," said Caradoc, a tremor in his own firm voice.

"That was what I meant. That's why I bolted —that and——"

"I know. Know, by Jove? I understand— everything!"

"What do you think you understand?"

And at last the brown eyes met his, drowned in their shame, but so keenly inquisitive that, to the male mind, their look was a confirmation in itself.

"I understand," he said, "why I've liked you so much in spite of your unmanliness. It was *because* of it—all the time!"

"But you won't like me any more!"

"Won't I?" And the bracken broke before his stride—broke louder than his hurried, whispered words.

"What are you givin' us?" There spoke the larrikin of old days. "It ain't true!"

"But it is; it must have been true all along, without my knowing it. I swear it is now."

"It'll dish you up!"

"I don't think it. The Archdeacon will forgive me; he's a man himself, the most sympathetic of men. Besides, I needn't go back to him; there are other fields. But—you? Is it—isn't it—true of *you*? "

The answer came with the last red beams of the dying day, in the first hush of the twilight forest :

" *My* word ! "

And now all that remains of that romance is a genial rector in the Old Country, with a wife who is not the less popular for being considered just a little Colonial by the County.

THE MAN FROM BOT'NY;

OR THE QUANDARY OF A COLONIAL HISORIAN

BY ARTHUR PATCHETT MARTIN

THE MAN FROM BOT"NY:

OR THE QUANDARY OF A COLONIAL HISTORIAN

BY ARTHUR PATCHETT MARTIN

[Whilst engaged on the "Life" of Robert Lowe, Lord Sherbrooke, and on a "Memoir" of his early New South Wales rival, William Charles Wentworth, "the Australian Patriot," I attempted to check the blunders of the printed records by the living witness of some old colonial Pioneer, who might haply recall the scenes of the old Sydney Legislative Council of 1843–1850. After weary years of vain searching, I at last found him.]

" WELL ! I tells yer," said he, "I knowed 'em
both."
(As he lolled in my study chair.)
" There wos Bill wot squinted, and rapped out an
oath,
And Bob, with his snow-white hair."

Ho ! ho ! I chuckled, and brimmed up his can,
And passed him my best clay pipe :
I've found him all right, the identical man—
The last of the old Bush type !

And I murmured—"O ! Bushman of aspect weird,
With your tales of the long, long ago,
I'd fall down and worship your chest-sweeping beard,
If you tell me of Wentworth and Lowe ! "

"Ah, Sonny," said he, "they wos two good men, .
  And I misses their company still !
Bob was a brother— But pass *me* the pen,
  And I'll reel off a hepic on Bill !"

(And I thought all the while, how Freeman or Froude
  Would have dubbed it a wild burlesque,
Had he seen my "Authority," slangy and crude,
  With his boots on the top of my desk.)

"As to white-headed Bob—which his name were
    Lowe,
  Why, they went and made him a Dook,
Or a Hearl, or a summut—leastways, I know
  They changed him inter Sher—brooke.

"But Bill, with his squint, were a diff'rent bloke,
  As this story will give you a hint."
Then he poured forth an ancient and fish-like joke
  No Editor living could print !

"Lord love yer," said he, as he emptied his can,
  "I could fill up your book with them tales.
—I'm the Downright Genu-wine, Sunburnt Man
  From Bot'ny, wots now Noo South Wales."

.   .   .   .

When he'd finished his pipe, and likewise more beer,
  I turned to my notes with a sob :
For I found that this garrulous Bush pioneer
  Knew *nothing* of "Bill" or of "Bob !"

"HIS LUCK"

BY LALA FISHER

[09]

"HIS LUCK"

BY LALA FISHER

THE thermometer registered 110° in the shade on the day that Eric Dowling left Rockhampton for *Wanteroo*, which station, with its two artesian bores and immense run belonged to his wealthy uncle, Jackson Belville. But, as he swung along in an easy canter, his mind and heart were too full of happy thoughts to allow so small a trifle as the heat to trouble him. He was engaged to his cousin Helen Belville, and he was on his way to the station because his uncle had given him the managership of it. For three days he rode on, stopping at the different stations for the nights' rests, until, at about dusk on the third evening, he judged he was within ten miles of *Wanteroo*. His horse was almost done, and it needed his utmost efforts to make it keep going at any pace quicker than a walk. The country through which he was now travelling was very densely timbered, and as the darkness gathered round him, he found it necessary to guide his horse most cautiously between the trees, and to constantly stretch forth his hand to intercept any treacherous vine which, creeping from one tree to another, would, if not put aside, probably unseat him. He journeyed slowly on, a misgiving gradually strengthening in his heart that he had lost his way, when suddenly he saw a faint light flickering in the distance. He gave vent to a sharp exclamation of relief, and hurried his jaded nag towards it. He saw that it was only a small house—probably a boundary rider's hut. The light which had attracted him shone through a large uncovered window. Eric drew rein and listened, but could hear no sound within. Drawing nearer, he dismounted and walked up to the window. Inside, on a square slab table, a slush lamp was burning, and by the side of a huge fireplace, in whose centre lay a few hot cinders, a man was sitting, his face hidden dejectedly in his hand. He was evidently the sole occupant of the hut, for a single tin plate and pannikin were lying upon the bunk at his right-hand side. This bunk was an immense one, indeed, it was twice the size or an ordinary double bedstead. It was covered with a pair of coarse grey Government blankets, and at the head were three pillows encased in sacking. The chair on which the man sat, the table, and this bunk, formed the only furniture in the house, with the exception of a little three-legged stool, overturned in the far corner. After two or three searching glances all round the room, during which the occupant never moved, Eric called out, and without waiting for a reply he strode to the door and entered. The man's head was suddenly raised. The face, which was that of quite a young man, was deathly white, with what Eric believed to be mortal fear. One hand was outstretched as though in pleading—or was it warning?

"Don't be startled," Eric said. "It's only a poor

devil who's bushed," and he walked towards him. The man half rose and seemed about to speak, but the words died in his throat, and he settled into his seat again, and Eric continued, " Can you tell me how far it is to ' *Wanteroo* ' and in which direction ? I reckon it's about ten miles off, but somehow I can't make out the lay of the land." The man seemed again about to answer, but changed his mind and kept silence, looking Eric slowly over from head to foot.

" How far is it ? " Eric repeated a little irritably. " Are you deaf, mate ? "

At last an answer was spoken in a voice singularly rich and well-cultivated.

" You are very far out of your road, lad. It's a matter of thirty miles to the station, and it lies to the west from here."

" Thirty miles ! " Eric echoed in dismay. " Then I suppose I must camp here ; I am dead beat, and so's my horse. I'll go out and let him go." So saying, Eric turned away to unsaddle and hopple his horse. When he returned the " hatter," as he mentally termed him, was gazing into the red ashes in an abstracted manner.

" Some poor wretch of a shepherd," Eric thought. " Evidently a bit off his chump. No matter, I couldn't have ridden further. What a fool I was to miss the way. Got anything to eat ? " he continued aloud. " I've ridden some sixty miles since daybreak, and I'm famished."

The man pointed to a shelf high up on the wall. There Eric found a collection of groceries, a large junk of salt beef, some damper, flour, jam, three bottles of pickles, a small calico bag of sugar, and the same of tea, a large tin fire-blackened billy, and a small tin dish. He took down the billy, which he found was half full of cold sweetened tea. He cut off a large slice of salt beef, which he placed between two thick slices of damper. He took the pannikin from the bunk and filled it from the billy, and then, catching up the three-legged stool for a seat near the smouldering embers, he began his meal.

Neither man spoke for some time, Eric being fully engaged in satisfying his hunger, and his companion gazing moodily into space. When he had finished, Eric rose and went to the window. The light breeze had freshened and bore promise of coming rain. "Going to be a storm," he remarked. "There's very heavy lightning about three miles off."

The man rose slowly to his feet and joined Eric, who now for the first time perceived that he had but one arm, the right coat-sleeve hanging limply from the shoulder.

"The first for months," he answered. "It's badly wanted ; the creek is getting low," and then his voice dropped into the most mournful and intensely sad cadence that Eric had ever heard. "God ! how I *love* a storm. It takes my thoughts out of *this* world, which is hell unutterable, and it speaks of rest after fury, of peace after pain, in other words, of the heaven in which I cannot believe." He spoke bitterly and sadly, and Eric gazed at him with a new interest. They stood chatting for an hour on every conceivable subject, on most of which Eric found the stranger remarkably well-informed. Then from one thing to another the subject of murder cropped up. They argued about capital punishment for this offence for some moments and then, "I want to hear your opinion of the worst murder you think possible," Eric's companion asked. "Is it the more murder to slay a creature in hot blood; to shoot a man for the money that is about his person and you are starving; to kill a woman for love, for jealousy; to stab a man for betraying one's sister, one's wife; or to frame laws that banish a man from the face of civilisation, that hunt him from his kindred, and that embitter his wretched life with a relentless cruelty and a never-ending persecution—*all this* through no fault of his own. Which of these is the foulest murder, think you? To kill a man at once mercifully with bullet or knife, or to kill him by inches, first blighting every good that is in him—his heart, his belief, and his intellect?"

The words raced from the man's lips in a torrent of passionate excitement, even in a tone of accusation; but the storm, which had been working gradually nearer, now burst and effectually prevented Eric's reply to his extraordinary outburst. The lightning was blindingly vivid and the heavy clashes of thunder made conversation a matter of impossibility. As they stood silent, the man with a sudden, unexpected movement placed his one hand on Eric's shoulder. Eric's blood ran cold, and he turned and looked into his companion's face, made visible only by the lightning flashes, for the slush lamp had long ago been blown out by the wind. "*Mad*" was his first thought, and he involuntarily clenched his fists to protect himself. "Mad"—for the man's face was ghastly, his splendid dark eyes glowing like flame with some unnamable pain, and his lips working as though to speak, as though there was something that he must say. But as at first, the words never passed his lips. He conquered his impulse with an evident and mighty effort, dropped his hand, turned heavily away, and sat down by the lifeless ashes again.

"Before I turn in," Eric said presently, concluding that the poor wretch was either ill or harmlessly mad, "I'm going to have a smoke. Will you take a fill? Have you a pipe?"

- The man pulled a short old briarwood from a niche above one of the boards.

"It's a long time since I had a smoke," he said, with a sad half smile. "Thank you, I think I will."

Eric finished cutting himself a fill and then passed the stick of tobacco to his mate, who had risen and was now lying on the outside of the bunk, and soon the hut was full of fragrant smoke.

Outside the rain was falling in torrents, steadily and hard, and seemed likely to continue for hours. After half an hour's silence between the two men, Eric's smoke was over and he went to get into bed. He found his new mate already asleep and he, tired and worn out, tumbled over the other side of the great bunk, and was soon lulled by the rain into a deep and peaceful sleep. When he awoke the dawn was just breaking. He rose hurriedly, not waking his bed-fellow, and caught and saddled his horse. Entering the hut again, he left, contrary to all bush etiquette, a couple of sticks of tobacco and two sovereigns on the bunk next his companion's hand, which gleamed strangely white in the half light, had he noticed it. He tore a leaf from his pocket-book and wrote upon it, "From one whose luck is in," and placed it carefully beside the other things; and then he left for *Wanteroo*, in the direction the man had the night before indicated.

On the evening of the fourth day after his arrival, his uncle and he were sitting chatting and smoking on the verandah, when a stockman came up the steps and clanked along to Mr. Beville's chair, saying something to him in a low voice.

"Speak out man," said the squatter. "Tell me what's the matter."

"A stockman has just brought the intelligence that a man is dead on the outskirts of the run."

"Tut," said Mr. Beville. "Don't look so scared, man. He won't come here as a ghost." Then, as a sudden thought struck him, he too turned pale. "Send the man who brought the news to me at once," he said hastily. Presently a young man entered.

"Come here, Newnham. Is it true that the man is dead?"

"Yess-ir," Newnham answered. "I haven't ridden near there for nearly a month, but to-day I took the month's provisions to him. I could not make him hear from a distance, and so I thought I would go and see from the outside window whether anything was worse. He was lying on the bunk, and from all appearance he had been dead some days. There were two sticks of tobacco and some shining money at the side of his hand. I was very much scared at this, sir, as you may guess. I wondered who could have been there, and I rode straight home to tell you about it."

"Well, well, it's very sudden," Mr. Beville said in relieved tone; "but I'm glad the man is dead. It's better for him and safer for me. I hid him successfully for some time, but sooner or later the police were bound to find the poor wretch out. Very well, Newnham, you may go. I'll see to it myself that the hut, man, and all contents are carefully burned."

Eric's heart had almost stopped beating as the two men held this conversation. Why, horrible! his bedfellow was *dead* when he left him; but why were they all glad of his death? Eric asked his uncle about it in a voice so troubled as to be scarcely audible.

"Oh! its a secret, Eric—known only to a few of the station hands; but I will have no secrets from you. The poor devil came here nearly five months ago, hunted like a wild beast. He had escaped from an inclosure where he was being kept for a few days preparatory to being sent to Friday Island, and implored me to put a bullet into him rather than give him up. And so, after much thought and conscience trouble, I gave him that boundary rider's hut. Thirty miles from anywhere it is on my run, and out of the track, and I forbade *any one* to go within ten miles of it unless I sent them."

"But why all this precaution?" Eric asked, in the hoarse whisper of one who fears the worst.

"My dear boy, don't you understand? The poor fellow was a leper."

MY FRIENDS THE CANNIBALS

BY HUME NISBET

119

MY FRIENDS THE CANNIBALS

BY HUME NISBET

LIVING amongst the long silky grasses, with the rustling tatters of shed banana leaves intermixing, within the gardens of Kerepuna, the native coast capital of New Guinea, it is an easy transition of the mind to let centuries slip away in this equatorial home of unobstructed nature, as we have already allowed the many thousands of miles to go from us and the bustle and roar of that vast throbbing heart of civilisation, London.

Here I rest, afar from smoke and turmoil and all nerve-torturing inventions, on this winter afternoon of August—if it can be called winter, in this land of perpetual heat and glowing sun—under the deep shadow of a broad-leafed mammy-apple tree, which is again overshadowed by the lofty up-shooting, feathery topped betel and cocoa-nut palms that rub their bleached grey trunks against one another, and mingle their sap-green and sienna-tinted fronds together with a soft rustling whisper indescribably soothing, when it is joined to the distant murmuring of the ocean constantly fretting against the great barrier walls of coral.

The frayed ribbons of the nearly ripe bananas wave in front of me, and as they dip into the tall grasses and croton leaves, form delicious intersections of trellis work through which I can look towards the workers and loungers outside, some in cool shadow and others basking in the fierce golden lustre of those fiery beams.

It is a working day at Kerepuna; and as I walked along the streets, deserted by all save the young mothers nursing their dogs, pigs, and babies—for they are very impartial in their maternal duties, the sucking pigs and blind puppies getting equal share with the bronzy little cupids and cherubs; the very old females preparing the yams and taro for the home-coming of the workers; and here and there, within small sheds, mourners, all blackened over with plumbago, waiting with appalling patience over the thinly-covered remains of the dead relative, and guarding it from the attacks of the older village pets, as they wander about sniffing or grunting aimlessly amongst a perfect dog-and-pig elysium of perfumes, until attracted by some odour more particularly powerful and grateful to their nostrils; overhead, within the shadow of the eaves, the tame cockatoos perch like specs of snow, white upon the ivory tones of bleeching skulls—trophies of fierce battles and mementoes of more sickening feasts, there they hang over the doorways—of bistre shadows, while the birds chatter and break the general silence with the language they have acquired or their own original harsh screamings.

I feel glad to leave this almost deserted native city, with its five lofty spires and its picturesque, pile-raised huts, quaint though it is, for the groves where the workers are, and exchange the mortality-laden air for the heavy yet sweet atmosphere of the gardens—glad to fling myself down amongst the moist verdure after my hot walk over the burning sands and imagine myself two thousand years younger than I really am, if there be any truth in the creed of Buddha, and surrounded by the originals of those splendid antiques which the Greeks have left us as a constant reminder and reproach of our own physical degeneracy.

Here I find the gods all represented in the dusky crowd who have gathered about me, leaving their work, to inspect the stranger and compare the unwholesome colour of his skin with their own rich and satin limbs, completely nude gods, and nearly nude goddesses poising in unstudied and graceful attitudes, like perfect works of art freshly cast in bronze.

I can see Hercules, leaning upon his club, in the form of a Kerepuna brave nearly seven feet high, with limbs splendidly developed, and rounded shoulders, as he carelessly slouched with his mighty weight supported by a huge gnarled branch of gleaming cotton-tree, and his grave, good-tempered face, surmounted by clustering locks, bent forward. As he lazily examines me, an amused light smoulders in his dark brown eyes, while a humorous smile parts his finely curved lips, and reveals the only defect which I can perceive about him (though to him a special mark of attraction), teeth blackened by the habit of lime and betel chewing.

Apollo Belvidere, minus his mantle, leans with a wanton abandonment against a palm trunk, a boy of about sixteen, his carefully frizzled hair standing out a foot round his comely face like a golden frame—the dandies dye their dark tresses yellow, and wreathe them with scarlet blossoms of the hibiscus. He is ornamented with finely woven hair armlets, a necklet formed of polished human teeth, and a breast ornament made from carved black palm wood and decorated with boars' tusks, red beads, coral, and small shells, with an appendage fashioned like a fringe made from brown native-spun cloth, and the paradise bird feathers gathered at the base with links of minute shells. It is held round his neck by a braided and twisted hair band linked at regular intervals by the same shells, and with hollow nuts, which dangle from the ends and rattle as he moves. This ornament signifies him to be a lover or on the hunt for a wife, a priceless breast-plate which, as he lifts up the feather fringe and laughs to some young maiden while he reveals the tiny pocket behind, makes the brown cheeks glow with sudden crimson as she also laughs before darting away.

Young Apollo, I found out afterwards, has not fixed upon his wife, and is considered as bold and dissolute as he is beautiful ; the maidens like to look at him, but the parents watch his movements with jealous eyes, and he was at the moment that I lay admiring his subtle, lithe grace, impudently abusing the privilege of his love symbol. I thought there seemed more of subdued mischief than mildness or love in the lustrous long-lash shaded eyes.

Pan is also represented with his reed-pipes in the form of a middle-aged and somewhat undersized musician—that is, undersized when I left my own proportions out of the question, and compared him with the models beside him. He was half-hidden by the long grass, for he was a cripple, holding the pipes in one hand, while the other rested a stick on the iguana-covered top of a native drum ; but he was not then playing, for he, like the others, had paused to watch what my audacity would do next. I bought the reeds from him afterwards, with much tobacco, but the drum he would not part with.

I did not examine the female portion too closely, for jealous glances followed mine when they hovered near the vicinity of the " raumaus," or grass petticoats. The maidens were free enough of themselves, and did not limit their curiosity to distant glances, but gathered about me, and some even ventured to touch my arms and face with the tips of their fingers, after the fashion that we sometimes see ladies touch the leg of mutton or rib of roast which they are pricing, and this the fathers and brothers did not appear to mind so long as I lay carelessly looking skywards or at the warriors ; but if at a bolder touch I turned about to see the face belonging to the fingers, then I observed a clutch made at clubs and spears, and a sudden wrinkling of brows which warned me, as I valued the juxtaposition of flesh and bones as they had been originally bequeathed to me, that I had better confine my attentions to the male portion only ; yet I caught sufficient between these spear-clutchings and brow-bendings to satisfy myself that the women so jealously guarded, although possessing features and figures comely enough, are not to be compared to the exquisite proportions of their guardians. They are small, and tattoo their bodies from the neck to the waist with so close a pattern that they appear as if clad in a tight-fitting jersey woven in blue and brown, while their bunchy double raumaus, worn about the hips like a kilt, entirely spoils the contour of their lines. The nose ornaments, too, and the lobes of their ears weighed down nearly to the shoulders by heavy earrings of shells, require living up to from a New Guinea standpoint to regard as attractive. But they are lively and merry in their ways, when the first reserve has worn off, and leave all the decorum to their men folks, who appear to be well under their control.

As I cool down after my walk, we are becoming friendly, and by signs introducing ourselves, so that, by the time I have studied the group in detail, and they have satisfied their curiosity regarding me and become content as to my intentions, Hercules is by my side with his massive arm encircling my neck, while the others are treating me like a friend and brother instead of having me trussed for the pot—offering me the betel nut and the lime from their calabashes, which I chew with the gravity the occasion demands, while some of the dandy friends of Apollo get ready the "bau-bau," or native pipe, as the workers go back to their earth-scratching and taro-gathering, and we all prepare to spend a pleasant afternoon.

One youth spreads out a piece of native worked matting for my inspection, and as we trade for it with koko (tobacco), I cannot help admiring the variety and precision of the designs upon it as well as upon the lime calabashes and bau-baus—delicate designs and correct lines, over which great skill and true art taste is shown, as well as on the rich carvings of their canoe prows, paddles, wooden maces, swords, arrows, and axe handles ; and I marvel where this nation of naked and savage cannibals can have acquired their art education. These carvings are cut out entirely with sharpened flints and broken shells, for they have no iron instruments, or, at least, had none before the European traders ventured amongst them, and still prefer for ornamental work their original tools. I discover, as we become better able to understand each other, that great patience as well as great skill is required for the work. A vast amount of loving care is expended upon those weapons, and particularly their war implements ; the arrows, which are poisoned, being elaborated two or three feet from the fish or human bone tip. One bundle of arrows which I purchased from them, and which they carefully wrapped up for me so that I might not be scratched, were wonderful in variety, no two alike in design—dangerous treasures of savage art, as the poison is so virulent that the slightest piercing of the skin will cause a most painful and lingering death if not cauterised immediately. The poison with which they anoint the tips is procured from a decomposed corpse already poisoned, into which they dip their spears and arrows, while the idea for their designs is taken from animals or flowers, as the ancients did. This, with the happy knack which they have of seizing chance effects, such as a twist or knuckle in the wood, and turning it adroitly into some object to which they may fancy it bears a slight resemblance, gives the infinite variety, and reveals them to be possessed in a very high degree of the gift of imagination and poetry, as well as artistic power of adaptation and imitation.

Some of the arrows which I brought to England have a natural bend and projection ; these, when the signs are studied, present in some cases a hunchback, or a figure carrying a load, or, it may be, a pregnant female, or a figure with arms akimbo or crossed, as the natural formation seized the artist's fancy or sense of the humorous or ridiculous. Some represent snakes with the markings of the body freely translated into ornamental scroll-work ; the face and human figure are represented in a series of scrolls ; the eyes, nose, mouth, nipples, knees, &c., so many points and terminations. There are no rude or grotesque imitations as we see in other savage carvings, but an idea caught and elevated, or mystified, to bring out a hidden and significant meaning which may be read only by the initiated : and all this is the more to be admired in a nation of so-called savages, who prefer, while capable of ornamenting so highly and weaving so skilfully, to go entirely nude. They will not trade for the gaudy clothes which seem to attract the untutored eyes of other savage tribes, and make no attempt to cover themselves in any manner, except by ornament, and only seem to disfigure their women through the spirit of jealousy, which they are more susceptible to than any other nation with whom I have mixed. The male portions decorate their heads, and at times their arms and necks, most lavishly, so that a full-dressed warrior with his ornamental hair-comb, flower-wreath, necklace, nose-bar, armlets, and cassowary tufts, is both a splendid and formidable spectacle ; whereas the divine form of the woman is obscured by the tattooing, and rendered disproportionate by her bulging skirts. They also cut the tresses of the women close to the head, whereas the men are shown in the full perfection of nature, unconcealed and uncurbed. In their courtships beauty is not a question where the woman is concerned, but the man in that respect must be above reproach. He buys his wife only after she has chosen him, it may be from a dozen or two of other claimants, for though he may have wealth enough to satisfy the parents, if he has not beauty enough to please her he has no chance of succeeding ; and where the courted damsel can look for herself, and the suitor has no tailor to fall back upon for aid to conquer, her choice is no lottery ticket but a substantial reality.

I find also, as in the case of the matting, that the inspiration was drawn from the cloud forms. They look about them for an idea and, failing earth sub-jects, they will seize upon the curve of a passing cloud and idealise it to suit the symbols they are working out ; for in all they do they have grades, hidden meanings, or tales to tell; and they will not tell them more openly than they can avoid. If their meaning is significant enough to those whom they address they are content, but they strive very keenly after originality of treatment. I find also that their taste in colouring is subdued and refined on their houses, canoes, and other articles. I saw no discordant or gaudy contrasts ; red not too glaring is a favourite colour, red inclining to brown or crimson, never raw ; black and white with perhaps touches of yellow. I saw no blue at all, and no green except the unavoidable bluish shade which the tattoo markings leave upon the skin—this, with the rich copper-tint, makes a most harmonious contrast in low tones. Grey I find to be the general tone over all—houses, grasses, and foliage.

For the carvings upon their lime calabashes, war-shields, bau-baus, canoe prows, and latokoes they use a pointed firebrand, burning in the design when the calabashes are green, and drying them afterwards. Their matting they indent with a simple sharp-pointed stick while the moisture is still in the fibre, by which operation after it dries it becomes arabesqued and embossed, the indented portions drying a shade darker or lighter as the ray falls upon them.

It seems to be a curious circumstance that they should spend so much labour on the arrows, which they poison and only make use of on the rare occasions when the enemy is beyond their capture, and when, as a last resource, they throw those highly decorated shafts away without a hope of recovery. Certainly revenge is a passion which we weak mortals are apt to cherish as carefully as love, indeed, in many cases the passion lasts longer, and instead of abating with the gratification seems rather to increase in strength the longer it is cherished and the more it is fed. This may be some explanation; another may be that these decorations mean curses indelibly carved in the black wood and picked out with white. From what I know of the character of these natives, I incline to the opinion that where the figure of a man is designed it carries with it the anathema of the shooter and the doom of the receiver portrayed upon it; and where a snake is represented, as it is always depicted having its mouth open and the point emerging like a fang, it is a symbol of death; at any rate, with the deadly fluid with which it is anointed there can be no question as to the intention of its mission.

When they go out on an ordinary fighting expedition it is much in the same spirit as did our Border barons in the olden times—partly to avenge a death or return a raid from the rival tribe, and partly when their trading vessels come home unsuccessful, and they find their larder getting low. I dare say, to outsiders the idea of a cannibal is inexpressibly shocking and revolting ; but after living amongst them and discovering in them the same traits of honesty, honour, even chivalry, as might have been found in the beef-and-mutton-eating knights of old, this feeling of horror dies away ; and we can understand how a people may be cannibal through long custom and tradition without being innately more ferocious than the peaceful citizen who buys his steak or chop of the humane-looking, good-tempered butcher round the corner. Personally, although out of a purely disinterested friendship, I have been offered a piece of human broil, I never tasted it, but this I regarded as prejudice bred from custom entirely. As I might pause before I attempted beetle-pie, however delicately dressed up, also, if I could overcome this early prejudice, I would not, any more than the Papuan native cares to do, be induced to taste a European, knowing them and their failings as I do. Yet, except from that early prejudice, which will not be overcome, I do not know of any more reasonable objections which can be set up against a good, simple-living, moral, and healthy-fed savage, or even an opium-flavoured Chinaman (which, they tell me, is very sweet) than can be set up by vegetarians against the flesh of the ox, sheep, or pig. Of course, when it comes to the taking of life, then the same objection applies all round, and that is about the only philosophical objection which we can raise on the subject.

The New Guinea native in his hours of peace and friendship is all that can be desired—faithful, humane, courteous ; in his hours of wrath and revenge he is no more a demon than you will meet any day in civilised England. When he sets out on these expeditions of revenge and food-providing, he goes with the Border chief's set object of not risking more than he can avoid ; he sets out on the war-trail secretly and silently, watches for his opportunity when he may find the enemy unprepared, then he pounces upon him, pithing him with his man-trap, plunging his spear into him, and felling him with his club, and afterwards, like a prudent hunter, cuts him up into serviceable pieces, and carries him straightway home to utilise. If they are forced into battle they will fight boldly and fiercely; there is no giving way or surrender, the termination of the battle meaning that he either will have food, or be food ; his poisoned spears or arrows are not used here ; the hunting weapons, ordinary arrows, clubs, axes, spears, and man-traps, and both sides fight on equal terms, and with similar intentions. After a man has lived amongst them for a time he begins to think it rather a compliment to be considered good enough to eat. I did not feel very highly flattered when, after asking a native who was leisurely feeling my muscles if I was good ki-ki (food), he replied with rather a wry face : "No, no ; too salt ; no good. Chinaman very good."

Although very patient in their art labour, and showing no object of ornament as being too trivial for their care, upon their latokoes, or trading vessels, they lavish their very choicest workmanship.

These latokoes, or large trading vessels, represent

what man-of-war frigates do with us, or what an East Indiaman of the olden times was when there were pirates to be guarded against, as well as storms to encounter. For ordinary purposes, such as fishing, &c., they use single, mat-sailed canoes, each family possessing one and sometimes more, as they are great sailors and fishermen, as well as industrious in their gardens ; and these everyday canoes or catamarans, are fashioned as simply as is consistent with utility : a tree-trunk adzed-out and without riggers, composed of branches roped together, with a straight branch for the mast, and the matting stretched on to a frame of bamboo, and only a few fringes of dried palm fronds by way of streamers. The shape of these sails varies according to the particular fancy of each tribe— square-shaped, or on the upper edge, crescent-cut, with pointed horns. With these they can dash along at a great rate and with perfect safety, without danger of capsizing, even although appearing top-heavy, supported and held on to the water as they are by those wide-spreading out-riggers. The sail, being a fixture to the framework, has to be shifted bodily round when they want to tack, but this they manage with great dexterity.

But the latokoe is the property of the tribe, over the building of which years are spent, each individual carpenter contributing his labour, and all lavishly assisting to embellish and enrich. When not required it is safely placed high and dry in the most sheltered and shady spot, and carefully covered with matting. It is only brought out once a year, when the harvest is over and the long voyage westward is to be made for trading purposes ; and when that time comes it is the excitement of the village.

These latokoes are very large, the most stately being at times one hundred or two hundred feet long, with lofty platforms above the hull, where the steersman can sit high and dry, and the cargo may be carried securely. They have three sails, the tops being cut like a divided swallow-tail, and the bottom terminating in a sharp point, while from the edges stream long ribbons of palm fronds, and hair-made ropes, from which swing human and dog skulls, shells and tufts of the dark cassowary, or gayer plumage of the parrots, kingfishers, and paradise-bird, tails. These sails, although so immense as to spread, they are able to shift and veer about with the greatest rapidity, now upright, now broadways or upside down, as they wish to catch or avoid the passing air-currents.

Along the upper edge of the hull is a line of rich carving of about two feet in width, almost covered when they are sailing by fringes of shells and feathers, and the railings which they fasten to the frame of the outrigger, and to which they attach their cargo of taros, yams, bananas, cocoa-nuts, prepared fish, oyster-shells, skull trophies, carvings, and earthenware, the preparation and produce of a year, which they carry westward to the flat lands to barter for rice and sago.

At both ends of the ship are raised, highly-decorated prows, with flagstaffs and plume-sticks attached, which project boldly into the air above the upper deck. They have also sharp prongs running out from narrow platforms beyond the prows, with hand-rails fastened round these prongs to transfix the vessel they wish to board, and the narrow platform to be the gangway for the boarders. A complete latokoe is capable of holding two or three hundred passengers ; and when they go to sea the best fighting men are aboard, dressed in all their war accoutrements.

A brave sight it is when the sailing season has arrived, and the vessels from east and south capes, who are friendly with those of Kerepuna, come dashing through the reefs, and wait to pick up their consorts as they go along. Then there is to be seen some daring feats of seamanship and great competition in the get-up of the adventurers, while they show off their skill ashore with shooting and spear-throwing, engaging in friendly contests of wrestling on the sands, while the young women and old men look on and applaud or deride, the old women being too busily engaged cooking for the visitors to lift their eyes from the yam-plates.

Then the camp fires flare out at night and scare away the evil spirits, who fly back to the darkness of the close thickets, and the spirit mediums do a thriving trade with their grotesque masks and eerie perform- ances ; and young girls utter shrieks of pretended fright (for they don't believe a bit in these spirit mani- festations), and rush into the shady by-lanes, with the young braves after them, getting mixed up and lost amidst the dewy leafage, much after the same un- sophisticated manner that country nymphs are apt to do at the shows and fairs of Old England.

Next morning they are off by daybreak, with the loudly-expressed well-wishes of those left behind fol- lowing after them, their sharp points dashing the snowy foam on either side, and the flying fish and dolphins leading the way along the intersections of deep water between the coral reefs, their dark figures crowding the decks and platforms, some fishing with their many-pronged fishing spears and nets as they go along, while others attend to the cargo or get ready their weapons for the chance enemy.

With eyes sharp as eagles, few of the sea denziens who venture near the barges escape ; a sudden jab downwards of the prongs as the fishes hang over the sides and up comes the wriggling fish, to be quickly pitched on the embers of their pot-fires, broiled and devoured by those who are hungry. It is all a series of change, mirth, and excitement, the swinging about of sails and sea manœuvres, the creeking of grass cordage, beating of the drums, and whistling of the reed pipes. Time is not much object, for they know exactly how long it takes to travel, and how long that eastern simoon will last, so that as they pass along the shores they will bring to anchor anywhere that they see the volumes of smoke rising from behind the mangroves, to join in the walloby hunt if the natives are friends, or to challenge and fight the tribe who they think may be weakened by the absence of their warriors.

It is a freebooting expedition, a mercantile adventure, and a pleasure trip all combined, and their lusty spirits are boisterous and ready for any feat. Past the lofty mountains of Cloudy bay—the Astrolabe ranges, and the Owen Stanley giants, who rear up fourteen thousand feet among the clouds, like the Sierra Nevada mountains in summer, softly blue-grey, like a cobolt and Indian ink wash, with white clusters of vapour cumulus all about its precipitous sides, and breaking the harshness of the outlines with the nearer ranges, dim, purple, and deliciously cool in colour and soft in aërial effect; villages nestling on the sands with valleys of shadow behind, and deep gorges down which watercourses and the torrents pour in the rainy season—now dry and velvety with the heat fumes, and broken sharply upon by the waving palm-groves.

From these villages dart vessels to join the fleet passing outside, gliding over waters only enough ruffled to blur the reflections of the hills, and blend them with the whites and purples of the clouds above, transparent water through which the dazzling white and amber coral gleams emerald and brown, with the rose tints sparkling like amethyst under the piercing sun-shafts — such a scene of prismatic flashes and movement as might have maddened Turner in his latter days, when his soul grew blind to all else in its frantic desire to create a pigment from light; a scene where the pulses throb with fierce pleasure, and the blood courses through the veins as if electric-charged, while we feel the necessity either to shout out or else find an adversary to fight with. We cannot wait on the phlegmatic tenour of dull hatred; the spirits are too high, we can only close in and wrestle out of pure combative joyance.

On past Kapa-Kapa, Round Head, and Basilisk bay the fleet rushes, anchoring when and where they like, past Yule mountains, abrupt and table-topped; looking in for a night to exchange greetings with their friends at Arora Aremma, and get intelligence of the enemies who have passed; past Oiapu, Jokie, Lese, Deception bay, to Motu-Motu, and so on to the rice fields of the west, where they are expected, and where the foe lies sullenly at anchor, waiting for them until they discharge, re-load, and get once more to sea, with the stormy western monsoon behind and a favourable opportunity to attack and rob them of their cargo.

Oh, those olden sea-fights! Again revived, before steam took the poetry from them, and the belching of guns covered them up and transformed them into mere thunderstorms, when the Greeks rushed with sharp prows into the hulls of the clumsy Persians, and the sun went down with a red eye glaring on an ocean covered with wreckage; the moon half obscured behind banks of clouds, till it seems like a bleary watcher, looking on the latokoes rushing, foam-mantled, past the canoe-inverted like houses of Motu-Motu, to join in the conflict waging in the solemn silence of the swiftly-gathering twilight, out in the rough waters of the Papuan gulf.

The battle is going on fiercely there in the open sea, with the bars of gold and fragments of purple clouds hurrying on above; showers of arrows raining from one deck to the other as the vessels rush along, clutching each other with their graplings, and the flecks of froth leaping up and smiting the bare, brawny chests recklessly exposed to the flying shafts; the sacks of sago and rice are drinking in the red flood which pours from gaping mouths as the wounded and the dead lie supinely upon them, while their brothers use their bodies as a platform or barricade, and with awful yells of defiance stab with the spear and bend the bow.

So the darkness gathers them in, and amidst the whistling of winging shafts, blowing of conch shells, creaking of massive sails, rustling of streamers, swishing of waters, and cracking of rails, the shrieks of agony, or yells of rage, and moans of pain mingle as the chained ships fly like huge struggling birds out of sight

.   .   .   .   .

After all, perhaps, it is better to be lying this golden afternoon under the shadow of fruit trees than to be upon the latokoes out there in the open, with Hercules and Apollo both waiting upon me, and the lame god Pan tuning his pipes to the monotonous accompaniment of the drum.

Better to be lying backwards and watching the thin wreathes of smoke from my own pipe, and the apertures of the bau-bau as they floated softly upward and spread like fine gossamer over the lush, broad leaves above me, while every now and then, as the palm fringes move aside before the soft upper air-stream, a sun-ray darts in between the intersections and makes a splash of vivid colour, like a brilliant green-winged butterfly within the shadows.

Pleasant to lie with the crumpled, reed-like grasses for our pillow, and listen to those sounds of rustling eaves and distant surf-breaking, with the soothing sense that civilisation and all its vapid ceremonies are left behind, as we look upon our silent companions, for they do not keep up the art of conversation in these parts, but talk only when the spirit moves them, and sit, when not disposed for conversation, in that delightful ease of silence which refreshes like slumber —savage companions whose presence we do not feel, who do not seek either to amuse or be amused, and therefore who never bore. My giant friend pats me gently on the back now and then, with a tender touch that is infinitely soothing, while Apollo softly kicks up his heels as they both wait (with the rare patience which *ennui* cannot lay hold of) upon my inclination.

Outside in the clear spaces I can see the women bending down as they dig or hoe with their primitive tools, their lower limbs half-hidden in the *debris* which they are casting about them as they labour, with their baskets standing near at hand, empty or being filled. The nude figures of the men glisten like satin where the sun-lustre strikes their limbs—smooth, soft, and polished through constant bathing, as they move about helping the females, who appear to have more reality of purpose in their efforts than their assistants. To one of the cocoa-nut tree trunks I see a young man clinging, as he swiftly raises himself, with feet tied at the ankles, and embracing arms, to the laden top. He is climbing up to get me a young cocoa-nut, that I may drink. Behind the open patch, where the workers are filling in the afternoon with just sufficient exertions to make time pass pleasantly, spreads a sun-lighted intricacy of leafage and white trunks of palms. I look out from the shadow into the bewildering confusion of dancing lights, butterflies on the wing of every hue, like bright flowers ; floating insects with transparent pinions, catching on their translucent, delicately-veined surfaces the slanting ray in prismatic scintillations ; crotons with their speckled or varied striped leaves, orchids clinging to the dead branches of the eucalyptus and cotton trees, and flinging out lovely strange shapes and colours too delicate to be observed in the general glare, except by the observant eye, some of them shedding subtle perfumes as they wave to and fro—tender suggestions of perfumes to which we can fix no name.

The figures of workers and idlers pass before me like the creatures of a dream as I look with half-closed eyes upon them—women stooping under loaded kits, departing slowly, while some come forward with jaunty steps and deposit their emptied baskets on the ground which the others have abandoned ; men pretending to help, yet ever pausing to prepare the pipe, or being attracted by some other aim ; young girls with their water-pots going to the pond or wells, with the boy dandies strutting about them.

I have rested enough, and rise to return, for the sun rays have already begun to grow mellow, and the air feels cooler. My two friends rise as I do, and the giant, pointing to his back, lays hold of me as a boy might do a favourite kitten to hoist me up ; there is no use refusing this kindly offer, as before I can object I find myself sitting lady-fashion on the shoulder as comfortably as if I was on an easy chair, and then we set off towards the village, of which I now get an elevated view, with a dark-skinned, laughing crowd around us.

He slouches along leisurely, leaning on his club as if he had no weight upon his shoulders, and throwing a great shadow, like a hunchbacked Titan, far behind, with the young dandies following after, and the basket and water-jar laden women and girls in the rear, along the long, narrow lanes with the high bamboo and twig-wickered pallisades which divide the different gardens from the unredeemed woods, where the dry tendrils interlace so closely that there is no getting through, except by the tunnels made by the wild boar when he comes from his darkened lair. Over beyond the sands that divide the town from the thickets, I can see the dark blue line of turbulent ocean outside the reefs, with the unbroken fringe of foam, giving the distinct line of demarcation between fathomless depths and shallow beds where one may bathe without fear of the sharks, who cannot leap over that mighty, insect-built wall.

The sun is hanging in the west like a great orange-tinted Chinese lantern in a coloured space, seeming to be sucking back the light floods which he has so lavishly poured out all day, and the sand streets are grey with the shadow from the houses; but between the dark piles at the far end are glimpses of bright gold, and where an opening occurs wide enough between the houses, a broad line of the same glittering metal seems to be laid upon that violet-grey sand surface. The fishing-boats have come in with their freight, and are now lying high on the beach, fastened to the tall boats which rear above the thatch-covered roofs. On the platforms and verandahs tired figures recline, and carry on disjointed conversations with some neighbours across the streets. From many fires in front of the houses, where the food is being cooked, softly ascend volumes of purple vapours, which mix with the dim of the horizon and orange-crimson of the sun, the lemon-tinted flames sharpened from the contrast of the piles behind and the crouching figures who squat in front.

A rare confusion of figures, posts, flagstaffs, and streamers of palm-fronds greet my eyes as we approach : steeples bending at angles and rising sixty to two hundred feet from base to spire, with projecting bars and fluttering ribbons breaking the lines, till the scene looks like a gala day at home. Then, as I look, I am gently deposited on the high platform of the chief abode, and my two friends are explaining to a chattering mob that I am their guest and not a prize of war, while I wait upon the termination of the talk, speculating (as I see at my feet dark reddish stains on the silver-grey boards) what the last deposit has been here, whether trophies of the chase or prizes of revenge.

LENCHEN

BY MRS. CAFFYN

11

145

LENCHEN

BY MRS. CAFFYN

"AH!" she said at last, so soft and slow it might almost have been a sigh.

He looked down at her anxiously. The little note of pain in her voice chilled him. It went jarringly with the green delight of the woods, the stream's murmur, his fearless heart singing for joy.

"Lenchen, what is it?" he cried. "What is it, darling?"

She lifted her delicate, proud little face from the thymy bank to smile up at him.

But the courage just born in her smile chilled him further.

He resented it oddly. It was alien to his emotions; to the situation; to her sweet promise warm upon his lips, thrilling in his heart.

Courage in her at such a moment! It was a disturbing, unnecessary sort of interruption. It troubled his highest ego. It discomposed his manhood.

In this golden hour it should be all joy with her, all splendid, unconditional, abounding joy, even as it was with him.

"Lenchen! Lenchen, mine!"

"Albrecht!" she laughed softly, "poor Albrecht!" She looked up into his kind, strong face, and with her gentle gaze pierced straight to the trouble in his honest man's heart, as likewise to the ruffling of the equally virile spirit. And the causes of both, although to him as indefinable as they were incomprehensible, were to her quite crystal-clear. For the key to them lay in a subtle power of true vision, passed on to her through many a mother.

"Well, if you will, you will," said she, obeying through sheer force of habit the entreaty in his eyes. Then for one little second she paused to hold his hand tight to her heart.

"But words," she said, "are little fretting things; sometimes silence is better."

"Tell me, Lenchen, mine."

"Ach, Albrecht, what a man you are!" She laid her hands upon his arms, drew herself up by them, and stood beside him, slender, sweet, and fine. His blue eyes noted the majesty that made of her simple girlhood so rare a thing, and they flashed like proud male sapphires.

She saw the flash, and again she laughed; but her laugh died at birth, and a sudden wistfulness quenched the little hint of mockery in her grey eyes.

"I was wondering how it would be to be always on the edge of life," said she.

"But—but—Heart's beloved. How?"

"Can't you see? Oh, Albrecht, can't you see?" She stopped to read his perplexed face, to wonder at man, to realise the folly of words, yet, woman-like, to speak them. "You—you will plunge right into everything. You will see and know all things. You will also be seen and known by all." Here Albrecht perceptibly winced. "While I? Why I shall just wait here until you come back, to hear your report upon it; to have it translated for me. Also," she added with brilliant eyes, "also a little transposed!"

"But," he cried, "you will be with me in spirit, dear Heart's delight."

"Oh, yes! I was then wondering how the poor body would like that."

He watched her surprised.

"First-hand knowledge is delightful," she sighed.

She looked out into the twilight deepening to night in the dim shadow-land of the woods across the waters. She looked up at the little brown birds sailing in sleepy pairs to their scented homes. She leant her golden head against the silken silver bark of a young birch and bent her eyes to hide from them the confused dumb pain in Albrecht's.

"It was the wood that set me thinking," she pleaded. "To-day, when we went together into the heart of it, it seemed strange to think that only next week you will disappear into that other great wood of the world, alone; into all its delights, and depths, and hidden mysteries. And I shall just wait outside to see you go and come again."

"Isn't love enough, then?" he protested tenderly.

"Haven't I proved my faith in it?" said she.

But Albrecht still looked hurt. "And honour? That is satisfied."

He lifted his proud head, and bit his little beautiful moustache.

"That too! Between us, we being we, only that was possible."

"Your mother was wholly content and glad."

"So she was!　My mother is a saint who has seen her full.　She has also been seen her full."

"The world," he cried, at his wits' end.　"That other great wood of the world, as you call it, is full of dangers, of fears, of unutterable hideousness."

"The crowning delight of the wood," she murmured, "is the boar with the grizzly tusks that we know lies hid in it."

For a moment Albrecht stood stricken.　So gentle, so sweet, so child-like, and such an utterance!

"Lenchen.　Heart's dearest!" at last he faltered, his voice sounding stifled because of his keen pain. "Are you sorry?　Do you indeed regret?"

The bride of twenty days looked once more towards the woods, longingly.　Then her eyes returned to his face slowly, and rested there, as though they had found home.　Then she laughed out clear and radiant.

"No; I am glad, I am glad.　It's worth it," she cried; "it's worth it all!"

But by this time she had taken her lesson in man in an intelligent spirit, and knew pretty well how much he could stand.　She laid her soft pink cheek against Albrecht's breast, and made a little silent vow.　Had he seen the recurrence of that misdirected courage in her smile as she did so, Albrecht would, no doubt, have suffered another little shiver.　He perceived nothing, however, but a red ray of sun upon the gold of her hair, and the delicate round bend of her neck—utterly feminine combinations both, and soothing—the very sign and seal of her womanhood.

As they went home across the sleeping shadows, through the scents, fresh washed by the dew, and the songs which the hour made more tender—and the scents and the songs for them alone of all the world—Albrecht was thanking the Infinities, vague Teuton Infinities, their immensity veiled oddly under their homely swaddling clothes of sentiment, for the incomparable frail creature committed to his keeping.

He would prove himself worthy of all trust. He would guard his treasure as befitted his own honour, and her priceless worth.

It was a divine reflection. The heart of Albrecht swelled like a young god's. His face shone.

Then impish fancy strayed back to the ill-timed courage in that singular smile. The young man grew sedate and pondered. His child-bride was now and then a little discomposing.

Sweet, yielding, uncritical, true woman to her pure heart's core, yet could her eyes see oddly keen and far.

Albrecht's ideals hitherto had gone with half-closed lids—an attitude exceeding lovely and pleasant. What need for piercing vision with a man's trained eyes at beck and call? Wherefore any cry for strength, with an experienced arm in its proper position supporting weakness?

The thing was out of order.

At the last stiff climb up the sheer precipice that led to the old wood-embosomed castle on the crag, the spirits of Albrecht flowed back in full measure.

In the matter of climbing, Lenchen was ideal through and through. She now clung to him precisely as she ought to do always. A little trustful, swaying, panting, pathetic feather-weight.

Albrecht's kiss as he clasped her trembled with a new tenderness.

As for Lenchen, until the climb had absorbed the whole of her, she had been wondering how on earth she could ever manage to keep the vow she had imposed upon herself. And with each thought the proposed task grew but the more difficult.

Silence is good no doubt, and a discipline. But for herself Lenchen preferred speech. It was more simple and natural, and she was essentially a spontaneous girl this Lenchen.

Besides being of the blood royal, hereditary highnesses in their own right, the family of Albrecht—a stoical race—had for untold generations married into other hereditary highnesses of the blood unblendingly. An incredible number of quarterings, therefore, graced Albrecht's shield, and he had many responsibilities. These he took seriously and in order, and with unmurmuring fortitude attacked each in its kind.

He married, when twenty, another hereditary highness, with freckles and an uneven temper, and secured the succession.

Having drawn a hard breath or two, he then put aside morbidity, re-ordered his points of view, and remaining faithful to his wife, tried his best to endure her gracefully; also when a merciful consumption brought peace, to experience a reasonable degree of sorrow.

The boy inherited many of the attributes of his mother, and was hardly a son wholly to fill the heart of a father of six-and-twenty.

Having regard to this fact, the relatives of Albrecht being, despite their exalted sphere, but human, made a plentiful provision of marriageable hereditary highnesses, as good-looking as was at the moment possible, wherewith they hemmed him in on every side.

Possibly they overdid it.

At any rate, Albrecht broke loose one day, and showed a disposition to seek solace amongst less exalted ladies.

The relaxation was but of short duration. For one summer's day he met Lenchen. And after that he respected all women, and loved one.

Lenchen was the daughter of a petty baron, with only a trifle of seven quarterings to his shield. There was not a trace of hereditary highness anywhere about her. And this was unfortunate, for in her heart she was a queen, pure and simple, and she looked it.

But what availed that with the blood royal in the way?

There are means, however, to circumvent even the blood royal, and a man's left hand may be as sure a shield and defence as his right, if only his heart be true. The thing is done daily, and custom makes morality.

Thus Albrecht felt no less chivalrous than usual, when, in a flood of harvest moonlight, he made a fervent and poetic offering of the wrong hand to his heart's beloved.

As for Lenchen, she hardly knew, so dearly did she love Albrecht, how the slight anomaly in the transaction struck her.

The old baron and his saintly wife had already, with a sagacity and swiftness almost miraculous, recognised the truth that lay in Albrecht, the Hereditary Prince of Schwallenberg. This fact, combined with their profound and pious belief in the blood, carried them over the fence gallantly. It is indeed doubtful, so high soared the paternal emotions, if they were conscious of any fence to be crossed.

They wept certainly at the wedding freely. Given their age and atmosphere, they could not well have done otherwise. But no trace of misgiving, still less of shame, did there enter into these tears to interfere with their restful balm.

Lenchen went forth from the home of her ancestors crowned with pious blessings.

The leanness of sorrow brings thought to the host; the fulness of joy to a little handful.

Lenchen found it one day when her delight had grown so keen that it hurt her.

She was tired a little after all those long hot, lovely days with Albrecht beside the waters, amidst the woods. And so, when he was called away to meet a messenger from the outer world, she stayed in her place to think of her happiness.

This was to hazard a great deal; for happiness is too delicate and shy a thing to be dissected. The touches of women upon their own affairs, however tender, partake always a little of the scalpel-knife, and happiness being a fine, timid thing, is easily startled.

Also to be alone amidst green trees, beside running waters, brings truth too close.

Presently the beckoning mystery of the woods and the beckoning mystery of the world got curiously jumbled in Lenchen's brain; while, with Albrecht's out of the way, it grew quite an easy matter to believe in the reality of her own divine rights and his assertions concerning them. For the first time in her short life, Lenchen was clearly conscious that she too had been made to reign.

She was aware of herself. She was quite wide-awake.

A thousand new points of view sprang up like live flames in the rich young heart of the girl.

Albrecht was as sensitive as he was proud, and all that scented morning he had been telling his young wife of all the beautiful arrangements he had been making on her behalf. And so long as her head had lain upon his breast, just so long had his intense masculinity carried her with it.

His superb sense of responsibility had touched and thrilled her exquisitely. She felt as she always did when half-way up the precipice, ready to throw herself joyously upon his strength.

And indeed nothing could have sounded more alluring than did Albrecht's plans. And his voice could any day transform an Amazon into a slave. He had a gift in that direction.

He was so thorough too, no smallest detail had been forgotten ; while in the great things his generosity shone resplendent.

That very hour had he presented her with the title-deeds of the Schloss Rehberg. The yellow roll of parchment lay even now across her feet.

Rehberg should be their home. Amongst its woods, beside its waters, would they garner every joy of heaven, and with a touch of earth make each endurable.

Together in these terraced gardens, under the white guelder roses, would they learn of all wisdom ; Albrecht keeping one little step in advance in order to sweep from her path any dross unsuitable to the feminine understanding.

Albrecht's manner of putting these delicate matters was inimitable.

Never should the base world come nearer to disturb their ecstacy than the little red roofs of Bayreuth twinkling out through their green trees, just visible from the grassed steps that led to the rose garden. Rehberg was from henceforth to be for Albrecht home and hope and love and peace, the heart of life the centre of growth.

There were certain official hours, however, which must be won through worthily elsewhere; likewise a little unloved son to be tenderly entreated and made one day into a man and a king. These things also must take place elsewhere.

Here Albrecht had looked at his young wife and sighed. He was thinking of the sweet untried mother's heart, so ready to throb for that little son and sterilise the alien blood in him. But remembering its degree, when just upon the verge of cursing it, Albrecht paused and felt surprised at his impious lapse.

As he returned from his official audience Albrecht was re-ordering his wild imaginings and making a thousand tender, yet reasonable, resolves. In his new sketch of life there was to be no tampering with the right. *Noblesse oblige* was the motto of his tribe. A guide as sure as it was unflinching, and unswervingly would he follow it. Yes! For all the years to come must he parcel out his hours with mathematical conscientiousness, must seek heaven in one Schloss, suffer earth in the other.

Above all he must guard his Lenchen as befitted his manhood. At all costs must he spare her any breath of misapprehension; keep her unspotted from the world. True, it was not every man that took his morganatic wife or her position thus seriously. But then Albrecht was not as other men. He came, moreover, of a family of high ideals ; more especially in regard to the treatment of interlopers within their ranks.

And a woman's guarded life ! In good sooth it was a beautiful thing to contemplate. It thrilled and developed the highest and best in a man. Merely to think of it was a liberal education.

At this moment Lenchen stood up to meet him, with all the prickings of a queen in her.

But since the first-fruits of her sovereign power was a budding knowledge of Man, after her one little vague protest, she kept her vow faithfully.

And if there did come faltering moments in Albrecht's triumphant life wherein he caught glimpses of some disturbing note of interrogation somewhere, being, for a man, happily constituted, he seemed always able to cast it out upon the heap of other world-tainted interruptions he laid down always outside the threshold of home.

.   .   .   .   .

And so Albrecht came and went. He came to rest and refresh himself. He came to grow and learn. But of this he was happily unconscious. It were indeed a hard and bitter Providence that had made it quite clear to Albrecht patiently cultivating Lenchen's simple mind that the kingliness that grew in him with each year, the high purpose and resolve, the splendid potency and the gentle heart, were gathered mostly in the old terraced gardens beside his morganatic wife.

Perhaps the only good seed that sprouted but faintly

in Albrecht was his sense of humour. That possibly
was Lenchen's fault, for she neglected to water it—at
first because she was herself too sad and foolish to
recognise any need for watering; and afterwards,
when she had grown wiser, she stayed her hand lest
Albrecht, when now too late, should see wherein and
how much he had hurt her.

And always when he went forth from her, although
her conquering spirit went with him, yet did her poor
little defeated body like the permanency of its stay at
home each day the less.

For, womanlike, the farther power made manifest
receded from her, only the dearer did it grow.

Meanwhile, in her beautiful retreat the years forgot
to touch her, and by her ever-fresh and fragrant youth
Albrecht knew that he had done well.

The odd thing was that although kept so lonely
and apart in loveliest seclusion, as the years passed
Lenchen's name became one to conjure with. Albrecht put this down to the adorable aloofness in her
position. Familiarity is the death of reverence.

There was always a fine, severe simplicity about
Albrecht's thoughts as applied to women.

But there were other causes at work in Lenchen's
canonisation. For it was nothing more exalted or
esoteric than her own little human hands and touches
while gathered to her the hearts of Albrecht's poor.
And it is always from out the hearts and mouths of
the poor that saints grow.

Not indeed that Lenchen experienced any conscious
hankerings after sainthood. An early and intimate
connection with the state had complicated life for her
somewhat too confusingly. But her heart was so big

that it could not be cramped half idle into any terraced garden permanently.

And as her own little babies were caught away from her one by one, each leaving behind it, for a token, its little lesson of pain and sweetness, and a more bitter ache for that other little creature who, being Albrecht's, was hers also, now being taught manners by his serene and hereditary kinsfolk, so unbearable grew the loneliness at last, and so difficult to conceal from Albrecht, that one day she paused to consider. And from fear grown meeker, she listened at last to the whisperings of God in her heart, and followed whither the whisper led.

For, given a woman who is in the soul of her a true queen, one day the call will come, and she must forth to find her kingdom.

Lenchen found hers in the hearts of Albrecht's poor.

.   .   .   .   .

Still the years went on and Albrecht's son learnt many courtly graces. He seemed, however, powerless to unlearn the quality of his mother. To thaw that out of him it needed the enduring warmth of sheltering love.

Perhaps the one inextinguishable sorrow of Albrecht's life was his son ; an abiding mute sorrow that breaks the life in a man.

And he had to bear it alone. It was hardly Lenchen's hand that could soothe this pain. Nor could he apologise to his haughty son for that wherein he had defrauded him. Even German sentiment could scarce venture upon such lengths as these.

Nothing being lost, however, all this may possibly go to the squaring of Albrecht's account upon that Great Day, and break for him the crushing shock of discovering himself in the end a prig.

One day a great sickness fell upon the Prince and he knew that it was the beginning of the long night.

Lenchen had been through life his star, so it was but natural that in death he should keep his eyes fixed steadfastly upon her. During that strange illuminating gaze he learnt a great deal. But as he was trying to tell her of it he died.

And thus it came to pass that Lenchen kept her regal vow of silence until the end.

Even as it came Albrecht's son arrived from a distant court.

He sent gentle messages to his father's widow. For Albrecht the younger was never out of order, and piqued himself upon his skill in manœuvring a delicate situation.

But he carried off his father's body to its official home, there to lie in reputable state, where self-respecting hereditary highnesses could do their duty by it.

The first and last and only time that Lenchen ever crossed the threshold of her husband's palace was the next night. She disdained to crave permission to watch openly beside her dead, which was indeed a sore disappointment to the dead man's son; for, ever gracious and thoughtful, he had given full directions for the lady's admission, with a masterly intuition, arranging hours and doors with a due regard to Lenchen's claims and his relatives' sensations.

Lenchen, however, asked neither leave nor ceremonial.

But when the night fell upon the first day of her widowhood, she drove through the dim aisles of the great trees across the parks, and dismounting, walked alone and unattended up the avenue of beeches, to kneel for the last time beside her dearest. And at the first flush of dawn she walked out again, through the stately hall, tall, straight, and fine, with the proud fires of courage all undimmed in her splendid eyes.

.   .   .   .   .

One day Lenchen put out her hands once more to pick up the threads of her shattered life, and her indiscretion no longer the cause of offence to any high well-born one, she found Albrecht's world, which, to give it its due, has a picturesque instinct, quite ready to find out things from *vivâ voce* examinations, conducted with all due honour to the central figure of an engaging romance now happily rendered innocuous.

But Lenchen preferred silence and the kingdom of her poor.

TO MY CIGARETTE

BY MARGARET THOMAS

AUTHOR OF "A SCAMPER THROUGH SPAIN
AND TANGIER," ETC., ETC.

TO MY CIGARETTE

BY MARGARET THOMAS

FRIENDS are changing, years are flying,
      Hopes are failing, love is dying.
Thou alone art faithful yet,
Cigarette, O cigarette.

Life's deceiving, fame betraying,
Nothing stays that's worth the staying.
Come and teach me to forget,
Cigarette, O cigarette.

Kiss me as thou knowest only ;
Kiss the smoker, sad and lonely,—
Truest kiss the poor may get,
Cigarette, O cigarette.

Upward, like thy fumes ascending,
All my soul with nature blending,
May I pass without regret,
Cigarette, O cigarette.

A SEXAGENARIAN IDYLL

BY OLIPHANT SMEATON

AUTHOR OF "BY ADVERSE WINDS,"
"OUR LADDIE," ETC., ETC.

A SEXAGENARIAN IDYLL

BY OLIPHANT SMEATON

"GIE'S owre my specs, Tibbie; I'll tak' a bit look owre the paper. No' that there's muckle intilt; I jalouse—my specs, wuman, my specs, no' my pipe. Losh save's a', Tibbie, ye're gettin' as deaf's a dead tyke.[1] Humph! but there's nane sae deaf as them that winna hear, I'm thinkin'."

"Ay, ay, Symie, my man, there's yer specs to ye. I ken I'm gettin' deaf, but we're no growin' younger, gudeman," replied Tibbie Tamson, with a heavy sigh, as she handed her husband his spectacles.

"Humph! wha said we were?" was the ungracious retort. "Keep yer gab steekit, gin ye dinna want to seem a born fule. God send ye mair sense, and me mair siller."

Tibbie said no more. But as her poor old fingers tremblingly pursued their task of knitting Symie's thick woollen *hoiss*, or stockings, which kept his feet so cosy and warm when he worked early and late in his little *mailing*,[2] more than one tear trickled silently down her cheeks, and dropped upon her work.

But she was used to this cruel treatment. The

---

[1] Tyke—Dog. [2] *Mailing*—Rented farm.

day had been when she resented it, and bitter, angry words passed between the couple. But that was in her young and foolish days. Many years ago Tibbie had seen her mistake, and silently endured what she could not mend.

Not that Symie was a cruel, hard-hearted man, with no soft place in his soul for better and holier influences to find a germing ground. His farm stock was better cared for than those of any other *mailer* in Nethercleuch. The sight of any cruelty towards the brute creation made his blood boil. To all the world, save Tibbie, Symie was ready to do a kindness when it did not involve the expenditure of money. He was of that cheap philanthropy which expends itself in words rather than deeds.

In the village of Kittlebinkie, adjoining which his little *mailing* or farm, of some sixty acres, was situated, Symie was looked upon as an honest, straightforward man, as regards all the cardinal virtues of the Decalogue. No one was more scrupulous in the observance of religious ordinances, public and private. He was an elder in the Free Kirk, was held in high esteem by the minister, the Rev. John Muirhead. Nay, though Symie had what he called "a fair scunner at Eraustian Estaubleeshments," the parish minister and he always passed a kindly word of greeting when they met, in which such an exchange of civilities as—

"It's a fine day, Mr. Thomson."

"Ay, it's jist sac, Maister Thrawnthrapple, it's unco gude for the braird," [1]—or, "for the lambin'"—or, "it's fine dry weather for the hair'st," [2] formed the staple of their intercourse.

---

[1] Braird—Young grain.　　　Hair'st—Harvest.

In a word, then, Symie Tamson of the Cleuch farm was a man of whom the tongue of popular report spoke well. If he was a little near, and counted his bawbees twice before parting with them, and never let a "saxpence go bang," like the historic Scotsman in London, without getting an adequate *quid pro quo* for it, well! was not that an illustration of Scottish thrift and prudence? Avarice is a relative term, you know, largely dependent on national characteristics and idiosyncrasies.

But within the castle of his own home, Symie was a different man altogether. His *bonhomie* and jocularity became sardonic sarcasm and thin-veiled insult. His was one of those natures that are not improved by having yielding spirits associated with them. In such minds, submissiveness, in place of suggesting considerateness and kindness, engender tyranny and scarcely-disguised contempt. Had Tibbie possessed a stronger and more unyielding temperament, with a tongue savouring of the quality of Xanthippe's, in all probability Symie, receiving as good as he gave, would, many long years ago, have learned to bridle his unruly member, and his wife would have been a happy, contented woman. But poor Tibbie, after the first few wild, hysterical outbursts against the unjust reflections and bitter speeches of her husband, in an unfortunate moment read Paul's advice in the Epistle to the Ephesians—"Wives, submit yourselves unto your own husbands as unto the Lord," in a sense far too literal, and from that moment her domestic martyrdom began. For forty-five years her long-drawn-out misery of uncongenial companionship had lasted.

Both of them were now within a few months of

reaching the three-score-and-ten stagepost in the journey of life. Symie was still full of vigour, strong, active, and sinewy. His massive frame and brawny limbs had lost but little of their original power. His complexion still retained much of its youthful ruddiness and colour. Though the frost of the sixties had powdered his hair with grey, and his eyesight required some little help of a night to read over the news in the *Courier*, these were the sole traces the flight of the years had as yet left on him.

With Tibbie it was different. Time had dealt hardly with her, and worry still more unkindly. Her parchment-like face, though still retaining traces, under her invariably spotless *mutch*,[1] of her former comeliness, in the large, soft, black eyes, and delicately shapen, mobile mouth, nevertheless evinced the footsteps of Time in numberless crow's-feet and wrinkles round the eyes and across the cheeks, and at the base of the chin. Her elasticity of step had long disappeared. Her limbs were frail, and trembled as though with incipient palsy. Her frame was slightly bent, and her hair was white as the unsmirched snowdrift. From outward evidence, Tibbie would be guessed the elder of the two, though in truth Symie was her senior by over six months.

The diverse treatment his wife and he had received from Father Time was a favourite topic for expatiation with Symie, on which occasions he would stretch out his massive limbs to their full extent, and, pointing to poor Tibbie's bent, attenuated frame, would say—

"Hech, but ye're a puir, fushionless, deein' craytur, Tibbie, wuman," whereupon Tibbie would smile and

---

[1] Mutch—Cap.

affect to laugh, while her heart was breaking over her husband's comparisons.

Hers was a nature gifted with an infinite capacity for loving. But at every turn it had been cribbed, cabined, and confined within itself, and prevented from shooting its tendrils around her husband. Of love Symie had never known a trace in his youthful days. He imagined Tibbie would make him a good housewife, and he married her. A better wife and a more careful manager he could not have had, though he always grumbled on principle over her extravagance, lest she should grow careless. All her girlish dreams of delicious wedded happiness had long since passed away into the dull mist of the past, leaving her a broken-hearted woman, bound to an uncongenial companion. For many long years, she prayed night and morning that God would remove her out of her misery. Then she thought that was sinful, and prayed for patience to bear her cross. For one word of endearing encouragement she would have risked her life, but that word never was granted to her. Had Providence willed that her maternal instincts should have been gratified by the care and tendance of children, her heart might have expanded into all the glorious fruition of full womanly development. But of family Symie and she had none, and thus she dragged her ever-lengthening chain of sorrow on throughout the years—a lonely, heartbroken woman, with all the possibilities of good in her crushed out by the cruelty of indifference, which inflicts a deeper wound on the heart than blows.

But at the time our narrative opens, one gleam of sunshine had thrown itself athwart Tibbie's path.

Symie's sister had died, leaving her only child, a little girl of some twelve years, to her brother's care. Symie gloomed and fretted, spoke of sending her to the "pairish," and of the bad seasons he had experienced. Then it was that Tibbie, for the first and last time in her life, took an independent stand.

"Shame on ye, Symie Tamson, to speak o' the pairish for ane sae sib [1] to ye as ye're ain sister's bairn. I tell 'ee, wee Beatie sall no gang to the pairish, though I hae to wark air and late for her masel'."

Symie muttered something about a "toom hoose bein' better than a bad tenant," but went out to "pit" his potatoes without making any further remark.

Presently little Beatie arrived, a pale, waxen-faced, dark-eyed child, preternaturally acute, and with a discretion far beyond her years. To the desolate heart of the poor orphan, Tibbie appeared in the light of an angel come from heaven to take the place of the mother she had lost. A mighty, absorbing affection presently sprang up in the little one's heart towards the kindly, affectionate, but broken-spirited old woman, who lavished on her all the pent-up wealth of maternal love for which she had been denied outlet or exercise on children of her own. Between the child and Tibbie a subtle bond of love was forged, which did much to soften the old woman's feelings towards life and its responsibilities. So deep was the love the child bore her new mother, that though she could not understand the full meaning of Symie's cutting speeches to his wife, a vague appreciation of their drift seemed to reach her young mind. Her flashing

[1] Sib—Nearly related.

eyes and flushed cheeks on more than one occasion caused him to suppress the bitter words even when on his lips, so reproachful were the looks he received from the little maid. Kinder and more considerate by far was Symie to his niece than to his wife. But not a caress could Beatie be induced to receive from him had he spoken harshly to Tibbie in her presence.

The end of this domestic martyrdom, however, was very near. To many of the neighbours Symie's mode of treating his wife was known. Though they honoured the sturdy honesty of the man, they reprobated his cruelty towards a woman whose patient weakness won their admiration. Only one ventured to condole with her on the subject. The attempt was made but once.

"Mause Pairtrick," said Tibbie indignantly, "ye mean weel, nae doot, and for that I winna be as hard on ye as I ocht to be: but dinna let me hear ye misca' ma gudeman in ma hearin' again, or you and me wull cuist oot. Let ilka ane mind their ain business. Ma gudeman an' me are weel eneuch."

Her silent endurance under prolonged provocation increased the sympathy for her in the village among those who knew her story. But they had to sympathise in secret, for no one had a more pronounced contempt than she for "greetin' gabbies," as she designated wives who carried their domestic sorrows out of doors.

A fine fresh October morning. The sun had just peeped over the eastern horizon, and was flooding the whole face of nature—mountain and meadow, wood and stream, valley and plain—with that joyous, sparkling effulgency of rich mellow light which renders sunrise a spectacle so infinitely exhilarating. Those leaves—well tanned to an autumnal brown—which the boisterous breath of the late equinoctial gales still left on the trees, were literally glistening under the kiss of the sun on their dewy surfaces. The birds, too, were hymning their morning orisons, as Symie stepped out on to the road in front of his cottage to take a breath of the morning air, while Tibbie was boiling the porridge.

A few paces from the door he found his old crony and neighbour, Jock Howieson, vigorously flogging a cart-horse, which jibbed at taking the brae leading into the village. Jock's horse was an obstinate brute, and its master's temper was none of the most placid.

Symie watched the struggle for a moment or two, then, as the strokes began to wax severe, he said, " I'm sayin', Jock, div'ee mind the words o' Solomon the son o' Dauvid, ' The richteous man regairdeth the life o' his beast '; or, as Mathy Henry pits it, ' The maircifu' man is maircifu' to his beast ' ? "

" Ay, man, is it sae ? But I'll be bund, Solomon the son o' Dauvid niver had tae drive a bawsend meer [1] like auld Nance there, whilk wad bunk at ilka thorn bush i' the road. But I'm sayin', Symie, syne ye've gien me a bit word frae Solomon the son o' Dauvid, I'll just be drappin' ye anither orra yin frae the Apostle Paul to the Corunthins, ' Let the husband render unto the wife due benevelence.' Symie Tamson, hae ye been daein' that a' yer life to Tibbie, ye're gudewife ? I'm thinkin' I'll just be steppin' on, Symie ; gee up, Bawsy."

Symie stood as though rooted to the spot. Never

---

[1] Bawsend meer—Whitefaced mare.

before had his persistent carping and sneering conduct towards Tibbie been revealed to him in a light so morally odious and reprehensible. For years past, so thoroughly had sarcasm and cavilling become a part of his daily intercourse with Tibbie, that he had lost his sense of moral distinction with regard to it, and failed to realise there was anything out of the common in the perpetual snarls and growls wherewith he persecuted his unfortunate partner. He walked back to the house a humbled man. But as yet it was not so much the realisation of his sin which troubled him as the fact that it was common talk in the village.

Tibbie met him in the trance, her usual feeble, deprecating smile on her lips.

"Come yer wa'as in by, Symie, the parridge is dished, an' yer bicker's stannin' waitin'. Are ye no' ready?"

The custom of years, combined with the latent feeling of blind indignation at her for being the innocent cause of making him appear in the wrong, induced him to catch her up sharply, as usual.

"Humph, and whaur d'ye jalouse[1] I wad be stravaigin'[2] to at this oor o' the day? Women and weans are aye witless."

Tibbie cowered under the rebuke, but it was wee Beatie who confronted Symie as he moved towards the kitchen table, and, with flashing eyes, thus addressed him—

"Uncle Symie, what for d'ye no' love God?"

"No' love God? the lassie's in a creel Wha tauld ye that, ma dawtie? I div love God."

[1] Jalouse—Suppose.   [2] Stravaigin'—Wandering.

"Weel, then, the Bible maun be wrang. For the Bible says in ma tex', 'By this sall a' men know that ye are My disciples if ye love ane anither.'"

"Weel, lassie, what aboot it?"

"Uncle Symie, ye dinna love Auntie Tibbie, or ye wadna speak to her the gait ye div; an' gin ye dinna love her, ye canna love God, for she's yer neeber, an' yer bidden love yer neeber as yersel'."

Symie started. A sharp answer to the little logician seemed on the tip of his tongue. But he did nothing more than pat her on the head, and remarked in a strange, constrained tone: "God gie ye grace wi' yer tongue, lass, for He's made it gleg [1] eneuch."

After supping a few spoonfuls of porridge and milk, he pushed the plate away, and signed Tibbie to give him a cup of tea. But he only sipped about one half its contents, and then, rising, left the room, muttering something about "A slow haund maks a sober fortin."

Tibbie had not broken her fast. The words of the child had at first filled her with a keen, fierce joy, succeeded, however, by an aching dread lest Symie should in his harshness visit wee Beatie's protest on herself by sending her away. Tibbie felt that then the light of her life would quite go out.

"O, ma dawtie," she cried, "never heed him. It's dist his way; gie intil 'm, dearie, or maybe he micht pairt us."

"Na, na, auntie, I'll gie intil nane o' him. He's aye prayin' to God to saften oor hard an' stoney hairts, an' to gie us hairts o' flesh. Wow! but the Cleuch millstane is saft tae his hairt."

[1] Cleg—Sharp.

Her aunt only sorrowfully shook her head. All that morning Tibbie went about her work with a dull feeling of terror gnawing at her heartstrings. Presently, as she was busy preparing dinner against Symie's return, she was startled by a loud knock at the front entrance—a most unusual occurrence. She hurried through the trance and threw open the door. Mr. Muirhead, the Free Kirk minister, stood without.

"C'wae in by, sir ; the gudeman's no' at hame, but he winna be lang, I'm thinkin'."

"Ah, my dear Mrs. Thomson—ahem—it's on his account—ahem—I'm here. I am very sorry——".

"Gudesakes, minister, whatten's wrang, what's cam' owre the gudeman ? Is he deid—O tell me, is he deid ? "

"O no, it's not so bad as that, Mrs. Thomson, but he received a bad shock of paralysis while working on the farm. Fortunately he was seen to fall by the inmates of Robert Dowie's cottage ; and they ran over to him. They are bringing him home now. Ah, here they are, I see ! "

Tibbie waited to hear no more. As fast as her poor old limbs would carry her, she hobbled out to meet the sad procession that was coming up the little garden.

Symie was lying helpless on the improvised stretcher. The only signs of life left in him were his eyes, which moved restlessly from side to side. Fortunately his speech was but little affected, and when Tibbie met the bearers, the tears streaming down her cheeks, Symie remarked, with a sort of dreary, hopeless attempt at jocularity—

"Hech, Tibbie, ma wuman, we'll be a bonny pair

o' bauchles, you an' me, noo. 'Tak' me in by, lads, the gudewife wull show'ee the road."

Tenderly and gently Symie Thomson was undressed and laid upon the bed from which he was never to rise. Then the doctor made his examination, during which his looks became increasingly grave. Finally he shook his head mournfully, and taking Tibbie by the hand, led her from the room.

"Eh, wow, doctor, I can jalouse yer news frae yer face ; ma gudeman's days o' acteevity are owre."

"Even so, Mrs. Thomson ; I cannot give you any hope it will ever be otherwise."

"Weel, weel, ' the Lord gave an' the Lord hath ta'en awa' ; blessed be the name of the Lord,'" said the old woman, as, amid her streaming tears, a sad sweet smile broke through, like April sunshine amid April showers. "It's no' a' sorrow, sir ; na, na ! God be thankit his life's been spared to me." Dr. Bolus turned hastily away to hide the suspicious moisture that was dimming his eyes.

And so their friends left them to begin that strange new life, wherein Tibbie, the frail one, was to undertake the active oversight of the farm, and Symie, the strong man who boasted of his strength, had to lie helpless, hand and foot alike, and inclined to rail bitterly against God's mysterious providence.

For some days he was very hard to live with. Of a truth, it seemed as though he were desirous of compensating for the enforced idleness of his limbs by the bitterness and venom of his speech. Nothing, seemingly, could be done correctly for him. Again and again Tibbie had to endure such speeches as—

"Hech me, ye're a' jist ettlin' to worry me. Hae ye

ony brains ava'? Neist to nae wife a gude ane's best, but that's no' ma lot. Ay, wives maun be had, be they gude or bad, but the bad anes are like a hunner to yin."

But though her tears fell plentifully enough in secret, Tibbie never wavered in her determination to keep a bright face and a stout heart when in the presence of her husband. His bitterest speeches only extorted from her a sweeter smile, and the words—

"Wheesht ye noo, ma dear, dinna fash yersel', an' I'll dae better neist time."

She engaged a man to work on the little farm, and making a virtue of a necessity, she developed traits of business, prudence, and foresight, that even astonished her husband, though he never bestowed on her that one word of praise and affection for which her soul hungered. Day by day she went over all the accounts with him, relating what she was doing, and humouring him in the idea he was still managing the farm.

Wee Beatie it was who again opened her uncle's eyes to the hidden treasure he possessed in his dear old wife. One day Symie called Tibbie, but no answer was returned. Again he called, and Beatie told him that auntie was having a sleep.

"Sleepin' in the broad daylicht ! ma certie, that's the gait to mannage a fairm ! Nae wonner a's ga'an to rack an' ruin. Eh, wow, but women are as mense-less as a tinkler's messan.[1] Ou, aye, a sillerless man gangs fast through the mercat, and, faith, we'll no' be lang afore we're i' that state' Sleepin' i' the daytime ! Gudesakes ! "

"Uncle Symie, ye're dist an auld haverel, an' div

[1] Menseless as a tinkler's messan—Greedy, and lazy as a tinker's cur.

ye think ilka body's as bad as yersel, an' as scodgie[1]?"

"Beatie, whatten are 'ee mintin at," said Symie angrily.

"Jist this, that puir auntie disna get to her bed a' nicht wi' workin' to keep the fairm ga'an. A' the kirnin', an' the bakin', an' the sautin', an' the smokin', she does through the nicht, sae that she can hae the hale day to spend wi' ye. Eh, wow, man, but ye're a puir, feckless, fushionless, discomfisht body, lying there, no' able to rax out yer ain elbuck, an' girnin' and grizlin' at yer puir wife, that's fashin' hersel' intil her grave aboot ye. What gars ye be sae snar-gabbet[2] to her, that wad gie her life for ye?"

"Beatie, ma dawtie, is that sae? It canna be, it canna be!" said Symie in an anxious tone. "Ma puir Tibbie. Yer sure it's true noo, Beatie lass? Does Tibbie wark a' nicht? God forgie me, God forgie me; but yer sure it's true, wee Beatie?"

"Losh, uncle, canna ye use yer ain een an' yer ain lugs?"

Symie said no more. Presumably he did use "his ain een and his ain lugs" that night when poor Tibbie imagined he was asleep. Be that as it may, on the following day, after work was over, Symie called her. His tone was more kindly and gentle than it had ever been before. Yet Tibbie had been repressed and downtrodden so long that she actually trembled and shook when she entered his presence.

"Did ye ca' me, Symie?"

"Ay, Tibbie lass. I'm fain to hae a bit crack wi' ye aboot some orra things."

---

[1] Scodgie—Suspicious.   [2] Snar-gabbet—Sharp tongued.

"Weel, Symie, say awa'." Poor Tibbie could scarcely speak with anxiety.

"Tibbie, ma dawtie, ye hae been the best o' wives to me, an Heeven kens I've no' been what I suld to ye; far frae it.   I'll no' be lang wi' ye noo tae fash ye."

The long expected words of endearment had come at last, and their effect, as they fell upon her weary, sorrow-burdened spirit, was like dew upon a dry, parched land.   Her whole nature seemed to revive under it.   The long distant days of their courtship seemed restored.   Timidly she took his withered, lifeless hand in hers, and feebly fondled and caressed it. But as yet she spoke not.

"Ah, Tibbie wuman, had I kenned a' I ken noo, what years o' blessed happiness we micht hae had ! But it wusna to be, Tibbie lass.   Wull ye forgie me for a' ma sins o' omission and commission ; for ma bad, bitter tongue, an' ma blin'ness to the gudeness o' the best o' wives ? "

But Tibbie was on her knees by his bedside, sobbing like a child.

" Symie, dinna speak like that, ye'll brak ma hairt ; ye've aye been a gude, kind husband tae me,"

"Na, na, Tibbie, jist the *contr'ary* lass, jist the *contr'ary*; but, oh, I'm wae for't a' noo !   Gie me a kiss lass ; it's lang syne we had oor last."

For the first time for a period exceeding by many years a quarter of a century, Tibbie's withered, aged lips were laid against those of her partner in a kiss of love.   The old woman's eyes, as they rested on her husband, seemed to glow with a beautiful love-light. All the anxious dread, and the look they used to have as of a hunted hare, had left them.   A pure, holy radiance, the reflex of the peace that reigned within her soul, shone from them. Her days of mourning were ended.

"Eh, Tibbie lass, but it's like auld days this, when I cam' a-coortin' ye. We'll hae some twa or three thegither yet, afore we pairt, jist to pree the joy we micht hae had a' through, gin it hadna been for ma wicked tongue. Read me a bit verse frae the 'Auld Buke,' lass ; the nicht's closin' in, an' I'm kind o' tired. But the morn's a noo day, an' we'll hae oor crack oot then."

"Whaur wull I read, Symie ? "

"Read us aboot the Noo Jerusalem, lass, an' the comin' o' the Maister, in the hinner en' o' the Revelations. Surely I come quickly ; Amen ; even sae, come Lord Jesus."

The old woman lit her lamp, and Symie composed himself to listen. Tibbie's voice was singularly musical and soothing, and there was little wonder that ere long a tear or two forced themselves through the closed lashes of Symie's eyes as she detailed the glories of that world he was so soon to see. When she reached the seventeenth verse and read, " The Spirit and the Bride say, Come : and let him that heareth, say Come : and let him that is athirst, Come, and whosoever will, let him take of the water of life freely," she heard her husband heave a gentle sigh. Tibbie stopped and looked up, then gently closed the book and knelt by the bedside. Already the morning of the new day had dawned for him. Symie Tamson had responded to the invitation of his Lord, and had passed into the presence of " The Maister ! "

HEIMWEH

BY LALA FISHER

HEIMWEH

BY LALA FISHER

THE silver sea creeps in to kiss
   The harbour's wooded edges,
And bears to ocean's wilderness
   The scent of may-sweet hedges.
The white-winged boats glide gently in,
   With scarce a breeze to guide them ;
While shyly-peeping stars begin
   And gem the waves beside them.

The fairy-petalled daisies close
   And on their stems lie sleeping ;
The perfume of a climbing rose
   Upon the night is creeping.
The music of a distant oar
   In rhythm soft is falling,
And from some tree-top on the shore
   A nightingale is calling.

'Tis sweet, and in my native land
   'Twould fill my heart with gladness ;
But here, upon an alien strand,
   Its sweetness breathes of sadness.

If I could hear the bell-bird's song
　Through this calm scene come ringing,
Awaking echoes all along
　In that divinest singing.

If I could hear the hushed, deep beat
　Of waves on lonely shorelands,
Or watch the red sun rise to greet
　The towering rugged forelands ;
If I could roam the fern-clad creek
　And lie in knee-deep grasses,
Where happy birds their loved ones seek
　In seldom-trodden passes.

If one wee branch of ti-tree bloom,
　Or wattle light and golden
Appearèd to me in the gloom
　With baby buds enfolden :
Such sweet and well-loved scenes would wake
　Now half forgot and sleeping
That oh ! my very heart would break
　With longing, love, and weeping.

THE INSIDE STATION

BY DOUGLAS SLADEN

THE INSIDE STATION

BY DOUGLAS SLADEN

I

"YOU Englishmen," said the girl, "are such cowards."

"You new chums," began the tall young fellow with bad teeth, and light eyes that were a little too prominent. He mumbled the rest ; he had caught an expression flitting over the Englishman's face, and he thought Kit might have been a little too sweeping.

"I'll finish it," she said, throwing a contemptuous glance at the last speaker.

"You new chums think yourselves too jolly clever."

"But I tell you, I saw them."

"A mirage, and a heated imagination !"

"This is an inside station ; there have been no blacks here for years," said the older man, with the bleached beard and the big brown blotches on the backs of his hands.

"I saw them, just at dusk. I was lying low for a platypus, and my hound began to growl. There were a lot of them, armed, and no gins, or children, or dogs."

"If I were on a new station," said the man with the blotched hands, "I might think something of it ; but this has been settled a long while, and one can easily be deceived at dusk, in that thick ti-tree by the river."

"Pure imagination," said the girl, and the man with the bad teeth grinned behind the Englishman's back. He had shifted his seat to curry favour with Kit, who despised him. Like every man within fifty miles, he was her slave; she was so plucky, so pretty, so witty, and had, in such a marked degree, the lithe grace of a bush-bred girl. Only the woman feeling was wanting; she would not tolerate attentions from any man, except such as a subject might offer to a queen, and these she took with an air of prerogative.

John Forest too had frankly fallen in love with her, and she hated him for it. She loathed him more than any man in Queensland. No one else had ever dared to propose to her. She felt that he had humiliated her. Except for the silky coils of glittering hair, twisted with careless grace low down on her neck, she looked from head to foot almost as much like a man as a woman.

Her dress was of light homespun tweed, with a short skirt and a loose boy's jacket. The silk cricketing shirt, which set off her fairness with its whiteness, was loose too.

Before the men turned in for the night, they went outside to look round. They could see nothing; it was a pitch dark night, and even the practised ear of a bushman could not detect an unusual sound, though there was not enough breeze to flap the tattered bark hanging on the stringy-barks round the house.

A couple of hours passed; Kit had not slept. She was a little uneasy, "I wish father was here," she said to herself. He was a better bushman than either of the three men, and she could not help confessing that he would, as a mere matter of courtesy to their guest, have looked into the matter. Besides, while he was away, there was no one in the house but herself and the two maids. The bachelors' quarters, where the overseer, and the manager, and Mr. Forest, during her father's absence, slept, were, as is not unusual in Australia, a little way down the garden, and the men's hut for the shepherds and their cook was a quarter of a mile away, on the other side of the stables.

Looking out of her window towards the river, she could have sworn that she saw for a moment ever such a little light. Could this be a fire-streak? She had never seen one at a distance. She would have liked to dress, but thought it would be cowardly. She would have given anything to be able to defy her pride. She was glad that there was no light in the room for the mirror to show in the proud blue eyes a look that had never been there before. She was actually asking herself why she had allowed her hate for the Englishman to prevent her telling the manager with the blotched hands, or the overseer, to take the shepherds and the dogs and see that everything was all right. The dogs, which would bark at a 'possum going into the poor little kitchen-garden, had not uttered a sound.

False pride prevented the two Australians—the old colonist and the young colonial—from taking the Englishman's warning. They did not even take their guns into their rooms from the gun-room, and there was not a lock in the house.

But Forest felt that the house would be attacked, and determined to prepare. His tennis-shoes would make less noise than boots. He was fully dressed; he loaded his revolver carefully, and buckled on a belt full of cartridges—they might have rattled in his pocket. He laid his rifle, loaded, and a box of rifle cartridges on his dressing-table. On such a dark night it might knock against something if he had to fly from the house. The long Mexican knife, sharp as a razor, which he used for skinning kangaroos, was worth a dozen rifles for fighting his way out. Some inspiration made him look at his chimney, a brick shaft about a couple of feet square, which had never received its chimney-pot. He reckoned the chance of a native sliding down the chimney and taking him in the rear. That there would be an attack he was morally certain. He even went so far as to go and wake the others and entreat them to arm; but they simply said, "Blacks be damned!" and turned round sulkily to sleep again. There was no fastening to the house door, because there are no ferocious carnivora in Australia.

Forest sat on his bed, he dared not even smoke, lest the red crater of his pipe should guide a waddy to his head. Though not long in Australia, he was a man trained to sport *all* his life; so he had a vigilant ear; and even on that silent night there was sound after sound which made the sweat on his forehead run cold. First, there was scratch, scratch, scratch. Could it be the blacks? Though all he had ever heard of them pointed to a swift rush, silent or with blood-curdling yells, when they came up to the house, he could not help picturing to himself that they had changed their habits, and were playing the stealthy burglar, till a squeak and a skelter reassured him that it was the native cats, who were suffered to make their home between the ceiling and the bark roof, because they were such unremitting scavengers.

He heard the mocking peal of a laughing jackass; it was so human, it must be a signal. He waited for the crackle of flames—the black fiends of the early days loved to creep up to a homestead and fire it, and spear the half-stifled whites as they rushed out.

The dead limb on the big tree over his chimney groaned—the creak of these dead limbs, rotten as touchwood, barely able to support their own weight, is horribly human. That must be the manager or the overseer waddied in their sleep. Now the rush must come.

He heard a man move—it was certainly a man—he listened for all his life, but could scarcely hear for the beatings of his own heart, as loud in seeming as the puffs of the engine dragging its train up the zigzags of the mountains. He could feel the sweat running down his spine in that agony of listening. Nothing came but stertorous snoring; it could only have been the young colonial turning in his sleep.

All at once he heard another sound, and he knew— he had never been more certain in his life—that this sound meant something, though it was, if anything, less pronounced than the former sounds.

About one o'clock, as far as he could judge, after the long vigil in which minutes had seemed like hours, he heard the stealthy tread which told him that at last he was face to face with a supreme moment. He rose silently and stood beside the door, with the long knife, which he had learned to use where he bought it, in his right hand. He judged that a people so cunning in stalking would send a single assassin to despatch him.

Only one man came. He struck him the fatal upward cut which, if the line is good, reaches the heart, no matter whether the victim be tall or short. He endured a moment of horrible agony. Would the man live a second—to cry out?—— The aim was true. He caught him in his arms and laid him on the bed almost in one movement, then he stole back to the door and listened for his life. There was evidently a crowd outside the house door. He could hear other voices at the windows, which he had taken the precaution of closing. The sweat rolled down his forehead. In desperation he thought of the chimney, and found that by putting his back and feet against opposite sides, he could walk up quite easily. What a providence that there was no chimney-pot! But how to get down unobserved and rescue or die for the girl who loathed and insulted him, but could not turn him from the idea that she was worth any amount of winning. One side of the house had neither door nor window; it faced the quarter from which the hot wind blew; the blacks, who had evidently taken observations beforehand, had left it unguarded. But to drop from the roof, even if he did not bring one of its bark shingles clattering down, meant certain discovery, and almost certain death. He felt something touch his side, instantly the keen blade was buried in it—in wood. It was a bough of the great stringy-bark, which overshadowed the house on this side. It took a terrible wrench, where every movement might dislodge a portion of the roof, to drag out the knife, but it put the idea into his mind of crawling along the bough and descending by the tree. Just at that moment, fortunately, the blacks found that there was a corpse on each bed, and rushed into the house. A worse fate was reserved for the high-spirited Kit and her maids. Forest darted to the big house to save them. He found Kit quivering with anxiety on the doorstep, but on her way to give them warning. There was no need to whisper what had happened.

"We must fly; are you ready?" He half expected her to refuse to go with him, or to waste precious seconds in preparations or perversity.

She simply whispered, "The river; take my hand; I know the way by night."

"The horses," he said; but as he spoke a broad flame leapt up from the stables, showing swarms of blacks all round, and at the girl's side a tall savage in the act of raising his waddy to brain her.

II

There was a moment of ghastly suspense. But the black fellow, thunder-struck by the calm courage with which the white woman awaited the blow, hesitated a moment, and in that moment the clean upward Mexican stab, made with the same motion as drawing the knife, had once more done its silent work.

"The servants," he whispered. Just then the servants rushed out at the back door with screams of murder and the like, with the whole pack of black fellows after them. From the prolonged screaming they were evidently not killed at once. It was beyond Forest's power to save them after they began to scream, but their screaming might save him and Kit by diverting pursuit till they had some start.

Had Kit tennis shoes too, he wondered; her feet made hardly a sound in the deep loam of the track. It was providential that they had always taken their horses to the river by the same cutting through the "ti-tree." Both knew that in the river lay their one chance of escape. On land they would be tracked down to a certainty by the bloodhound instinct of the blacks.

It was a mere apology for a river, not twenty feet wide when a "banker" was running and now in most places only a few inches deep. Still, it would tell no tales, and there was a township thirty miles down the river as the crow flies; but the river was full of loops. They knew they must go down stream anyhow to avoid traces like broken twigs floating back to their pursuers. The river, like most Australian rivers, had a mud bed: Kit gave a little sigh of relief as they entered the water. It was a tropical night; the blacks had chosen a day when the hot wind was blowing, so that their movements might be veiled in the whirl-winds of dust, and the white men's dogs be parched with thirst.

Mile after mile they sped with swift and stealthy stride. They did not run: they could not afford to risk a sprain or even to splash heavily. The wind had died away at nightfall, leaving a sultry calm, like that which precedes an earthquake.

Presently the water deepened quickly. She stopped and drew him back to her nervously.

"The river is too deep to wade for a long way below this," said Kit.

"I know it."

"What shall we do?"

"Could you find the track to the township in the dark ?   Perhaps we have a long enough start."

"Could you hold it if I put you on it ?"

"Why ?"

"Because you must leave me, I can go no further. Save yourself.   I will hide in one of the holes under the river bank along the deep pool.   When you reach the township gallop back with a rescue party and coo-ee.   I will answer if I have escaped."

"But if you fall into their hands ?"

"God help me !"

"I won't leave you.   We'll creep into a hole together, and if we are discovered I can use the last two shots in my revolver for ourselves.   The blacks may not come down so far, as there's no track to show which way we went.   They won't search many hours ; they'll be keen to get right away before the troopers are out."

"How can we find a hole that's big enough without leaving marks all along where we try ?"

"There's a hole about fifteen paces down, where that big half-bred hound of mine disappeared altogether the other day.   It must be dry, because he came out all dusty.   The entry's not very big, but I know it by a flat white stone right in its mouth."

"You'd much better save yourself and chance saving me," she said, not very graciously.

"Keep close to the edge," was all he answered ; "it gets deep very quickly."   As it was, he had to hold up his revolver and cartridges to prevent their getting wet.

He counted his paces.   When he judged he was at the right spot, he bent his head until it almost touched the ground and peered for the stone ; he was afraid to feel for it—they must not leave a finger mark more than they can help for the trackers. Presently he made out a faint glimmer of white in the pitch dark. The dust raised by the hot wind hung like a thick pall over the earth, shrouding every star in heaven.

" Will you crawl in first or shall I ? " said he.

" You ; you could shoot me if they came up before we both got in."

He crawled in on his belly, and once inside struck a match that she might see her way. He had a little silver box in his watch pocket, which had kept above water.

By its light he saw that the girl had bare, bleeding feet, and apparently had nothing on but her night-dress and a thin silk dust coat. Fortunately there was no risk of chill that night. Another match revealed that they were in a hollow of considerable area, though nowhere high enough for them to sit upright. It had evidently been eaten out by floods, which the sun-baked crust above defied. It was shaped like the concave of a flattish flat-fish shell. Neither of them felt inclined to go near the sides, they had such a snaky look. He found her a place that could not be seen from the entrance, and himself lay down in front of the entrance to listen.

" You can come here," she said coldly ; " you are not safe there."

" I must watch."

" Come here, I say."

He did not move.

" You imperil both of us," she insisted, in a rather different tone,

He felt that he had no right to do this. Besides, it was her wish, about the only wish she had ever expressed to him, and probably the last. So he crept beside her. But he felt in honour bound not to ingratiate himself.

All the long night they lay listening for footsteps. On such a still night they could have detected even a black fellow's light footfall far away on the hollow, echoing ground. But they could not afford to risk an unnecessary word. She asked briefly—

" What would two men do if they lay here afraid to speak ? "

" They would lay their hands on each other's shoulders."

" Please regard me as a man," she said coldly.

But the hand she laid upon his shoulder, with an absolute absence of emotion, was vibrant like a vigorous man's and, withal, the light hand of a graceful woman.

He endeavoured to inspire his hand with no expression but that of protectiveness. Thus they lay till morning.

   .   .   .   .   .

There is no dusk in Australia. Night falls and draws up again like changes of scenery at a theatre.

How open the whole cave seemed in the daylight, though the orifice had only just been large enough to admit them.

As the first rays of the sun shone into the cave a cold shiver struck them. From one of the flattened edges of the cave a huge black snake, warty, and black as coal above, and deep red on the belly, glided right over the place where Forest had lain at first and coiled himself on the flat stone to bask before the sun became too fierce. They kept still as death; even if it had been safe to use the revolver the snake could have sprung before it was drawn, and a bite from such a full-grown snake, where surgical aid was impossible, meant death in half an hour. If the blacks did not pass they could not leave the cave without using the revolver. Both knew that a snake is never so dangerous as when cut off from his hole. The minutes passed like months. A strange mesmerism came over Kit. As Forest watched the snake, revolver in hand, he lay on his side, with his legs drawn up, in the best position for moving quickly that the low roof allowed. He was of course back to her; insensibly she edged up to him until she moulded her knees into the hollows of his knees and rested her bosom against his shoulder blades, her hands laid upon his shoulders, her head against his neck. In this prolonged and awful anxiety she felt an imperious need of contact to give her the sense of companionship.

Presently—the Australian-born had a quicker ear than the Englishman—she detected the distant fall of many footsteps. Nearer and nearer they came, a few on the further bank, more over their heads. They must have found the footprints to the water and were trying the river up and down to see where the fugitives had struck away from it. When they came to the banks of the pool they halted, they were too uncivilised to know how white men dread a snaky-looking hole, and the banks were honeycombed. They looked sharply for a trail. Two or three noticed marks on the white stone; but there lay the great snake—six or seven feet of him—snakes do not fly from the silent-footed blacks as they do from the booted whites. They held a short conversation, one man demurring ; he picked up a stone and threw it against the white slab on which the snake lay.   It of course darted into the cave.   No sound came and apparently he was satisfied.   The tribe passed on.   The tension of those moments had been awful, but Forest was quite calm and resolved.   When the angry, frightened snake appeared at the cave's mouth, he felt certain that it would bite him ; but he reckoned on being able to keep it off Kit.   As the snake entered he raised himself to guard her, the movement gave it a fresh scare, but it fled into its hole instead of striking.

Kit was not afraid of snakes, they had been part of her bringing up; but it was terrible to lie all through a summer's day watching for the deadly monster.   It was not safe to emerge till nightfall.

Instinctively he left her side, and slid to the opening to watch.

"I asked you to regard me as a man," she whispered impatiently.   "If we were both men would you not be keeping as close to me as you could, to be out of observation ?   Where I am is the only part of the cave which is not open to the passer by.   Please regard me simply as a man."

He crept close, but was careful not to touch her, for daylight had revealed her bare feet, her scanty clothing. She was pale with tiredness ; but there was little trace of fear in her steadfast blue eyes, and on her lips there played, as she caught his eye, a little smile of pluck, which went straighter to his heart than the tenderest glance.

They had nothing to eat. They almost died of thirst; though they could hear water running within a yard or two. For though they had heard the footsteps die away, a scout might have been left. Perhaps the snake was watching them from his hole in terror. He did not come out; but they spent the day with one eye fixed on his hole.

Towards nightfall they slipped out and struck the road for the township. The sirocco had passed and the stars shone out with the brilliancy of a moon.

"I will carry you," he insisted, though weakened by the day's fast. His heart bled for the wounds on the beautiful bare feet. She refused impatiently; but after a while she said—

"You may carry me on your back as far as the road; I might snag my feet in the bush."

"Let me carry you in my arms."

"Would you carry another man in your arms? How often am I to ask you to regard me simply as a man?"

But he took her in his arms, and once there she lay still, simply trying to lighten his load, as a maimed man would for his carrier. The *abandon*, which was born of coldness, filled his veins with fire.

.   .   .   .   .

"Put me down now; here is the road."

"You're not heavy."

"It's ungentlemanly of you to persist in treating me as a woman when I have told you so plainly that I wish to be treated like a man. As I have to be with you so many hours, you might at least do what I ask you," she said indignantly.

"The dust is so deep it's like walking in sand," she added.

"You go on in front and sing out if you knock your feet against anything. I can follow exactly in your tracks."

"All right, but we had better keep silence, in case——" It was nearly six o'clock before they reached the house of a squatter friend, who was also a doctor, just outside the township, sorry objects, especially Kit, with her bare, bleeding feet, her hatless head, and the thin silk wrapper, draggled with wetting in the river and lying in the dust of the cave, which had nothing but a night-dress under it.

For the last two hours, from the time that daylight made it safe, she had been leaning on his arm to ease her feet. They were on a plain which the eye could sweep for miles. They could not see a trace of the blacks, and the township loomed up against the morning horizon. In the fulness of his heart at their delivery he began to talk hopefully and merrily. But she said that it was a strain even to listen when one was so wearied out. She would have liked to silence her thoughts.

"We will stop at Dr. Woffington's," she said, "Maggie Woffington will lend me her things ; she's about my size."

Dr. Woffington lived a mile or two outside the township, so as to combine practice with squatting. He was standing on his doorstep, just about to mount and visit a patient before breakfast.

"Jump on," he said to the boy as soon as he brought the horse round, "and ride in as hard as you can split ; tell Reed the trooper, and Mrs. Rose at the telegraph

office, to rouse the country. Then he turned to Kit
Pender.

"You know my daughter's room; she'll rig you
out."

The pursuing party, as the custom is in the Never
Never country, exterminated the whole tribe of blacks,
led to their camp by a woman of their own race.
The affair was apparently a vendetta, and this woman
the cause. A shepherd whom Mr. Pender had
recently engaged had abducted this girl from her
tribe. Fearing their vengeance if he continued in
their neighbourhood, he had left the " Never, Never "
and taken a billet on an inside station. The girl
whom he had abducted, made his drudge as well as
his mistress, had been sent down to the dam for water,
when her quick ear detected the approach of her
tribe. Knowing what she had to expect if she
was caught, she sprang on a horse that was at the
water and rode it barebacked at a gallop to the next
large station. Meanwhile her tribe stole on to the
men's huts and the stables. The men, unsuspecting
and unarmed, were easily waddied in their sleep.
The horses being perfectly useless to the blacks, but
invaluable to their pursuers, were speared. Almost
simultaneously others of the tribe fell upon the
bachelors' quarters. They left the women—whom
they knew to be alone—till the last, lest a chance
scream should make the men rush to the dreaded
rifles. They had laid their plans with diabolical
cunning. Scouts had been watching for days, who
had seen Mr. Pender ride away, and had noticed that
the gentlemen all slept in the bachelors' quarters.
When the avenging party reached the smouldering

ruins the silence of the dogs was soon explained. Forest had taken his hound at dusk to scent the platypus and Kit had taken out all the other dogs for exercise because it had been too hot to take them out during the day. This gave the blacks their chance ; with no dogs in to give the alarm it was easy to creep into the kennels unobserved and throw into the drinking troughs the crystals of strychnine scraped off the baits laid about the run for eagle-hawks and dingoes. The attitude of the stiffened corpses of the dogs showed the nature of the poison. It being a hot, windy day, the dogs lapped up every drain of water as soon as they came in, and were all dead soon after dark.

Before either Forest or Kit had awoke from the deep sleep which follows the relaxation of vigilance after many hours of peril, the pursuers had returned. There was a tribe the less of the fast-disappearing aborigines of Australia. It had been hanging about a day longer than is usual with black fellows on a raid. One of the tribe had probably discovered that there were two whites unaccounted for among the bodies, and the tribe had remained to hunt out these witnesses of the outrage. And yet, if these blacks were capable of thinking, they would have known that the trackers would assuredly hunt them down, witnesses or no witnesses.

With the avengers returned Kit's father—ill-news travels fast—overjoyed to find his beautiful young daughter safe and sound.

She was quite girlishly pretty as she returned his hungry embraces ; quite girlishly smiling in her gratitude to Forest as her father poured his thanks in a voice broken by strong emotion. But when her father, obeying a kindly dictate from within, left them, she froze up directly.

He was stunned when she asked him in a hard, dry voice, "Do you want to kiss me?" She probably intended him to be stunned, for she proceeded, "When a man puts a girl under a great obligation he generally expects to kiss her, doesn't he? I suppose saving a girl's life might be called putting her under an obligation."

"I don't want to kiss you on those terms."

"I am glad. Perhaps I was wrong. You see, I didn't know how a girl would act under the circumstances."

"It's lucky you're like you are," he said hoarsely. "If you were any other girl I should have to offer to marry you, to——"

"To save my good name? Yes, I understand."

"I didn't say that."

"You said enough."

"And that would be one for you and two for myself," he added, ruefully. "But I suppose you're man enough for them to be afraid to say such things about you? Man enough not to care for them, anyhow."

Did she blush? She spoke quite ungraciously.

"You needn't bother. Besides," she added, yet more bitterly, "you said it was a standing offer."

"So it is."

"You honour me," she said coldly. "Yes, you do honour me," she repeated, with more warmth, "for I suppose you're the only man who would marry me now." Then she chilled again. "But it's an honour of which I have never been ambitious, and I suppose I can do without it better than ever."

"Well, goodbye Miss Kit," he said, moving towards the door, "I'm going back to join the men now, to hear the parts they did not tell about the extermination of the tribe. I'm going south to-morrow. I'm not going to make your life miserable with blowing hot and cold, according as your gratitude or your resentment gets the upper hand for the time being."

"No, don't go," she said quickly. "I want to show my gratitude a little better before you go."

"I don't want your gratitude," he added simply. "I'd have done it for any woman gladly—for one of those poor servants we could not save—just as much as for you."

"Are you really going to-morrow?" she asked, coming to him.

"I must."

She took his hands and gave him her mouth, as any girl might have given it to the man who had loved her and saved her life, when he was leaving her for ever.

"Goodbye, John Forest—goodbye, John. Must it be goodbye? Won't you stay and let me try to be decent to you before you go?" she asked, still holding his hands.

"Not unless you promise to marry me."

"I haven't fought off marriage all these years to marry a man who——"

"A man who——"

"Oh, you stupid man! Why don't you tell me that you love me?"

.   .   .   .   .

"I don't think he ever told her—in so many words.

WHAT DID HE DO WITH THEM?

BY EDMUND STANSFELD RAWSON

WHAT DID HE DO WITH THEM?

BY EDMUND STANSFIELD RAWSON

IS it an old story? Possibly! yet it is worth re-telling. New stories are generally old, and new jokes have been better told in the olden days; even *Punch* himself admits that he never was as good as he used to be!

The long and wearisome Session was over. It had been agonisingly prolonged by the verbosity of the "wind bags" who, like the "cheap numerosity of a stage army," came on and on, and ever on—from afternoon to night, from night to day — until the reporters were maddened with the repetitions, and the country was sick unto death at delayed legislation. But they never wearied, those woeful wind bags. They dressed themselves in fresh garments seemingly, but the same minds, the same feelings, and the same speeches were painfully apparent throughout. They were paid for their labours, and were determined to earn the money.

The thermometer had reached a daily 100° in the shade, and a nightly never-below 80° stage; the streets of the city were blazing furnaces by day, and the mosquitoes were enjoying a full complement of meals by night.

Hugh Daventry had made his mark, a distinguished and ineffaceable mark on the annals of his colony. He had become a Minister, with the much-coveted prefix of Honourable to his name, and the rather less coveted privilege of answering hundreds of applications from clamouring constituents wanting billets for all of their families, J.P.-ships for themselves, and a general loan of money all round.

Now, Hugh was a man of letters —learned, and everlastingly learning. Touch him on any subject, from the deepest chaos of chemical compounds to the latest fad in economics ; from the most intricate arguments on bimetalism to the simple hen-and-eggs theory of modern socialism, and he was all there. With the ordinary conventionalities of life, however, he had nothing in common. If his boots were unblacked, or his collar unbuttoned, he never heeded. A gentle suggestion that a sky-blue necktie was hardly the sort of adornment in which to attend a funeral passed unnoticed. He would appear at breakfast in carpet slippers, foxes' heads on red grounds for choice, without any feeling of being still in his bedroom ; and would have cheerfully walked in Hyde Park at a Sunday parade, in a tall hat and tan boots, and with a short black pipe in his mouth, without the slightest sense of anything incongruous.

Society smiled and called him eccentric ; but when he raised his voice in the House and launched out in scathing sarcasms or rattling bursts of rhetoric, Society listened with eager attention and exclaimed: "This is our man—this is a genius!"

Gifted with a marvellous memory for every subject but conventionalism, is it to be wondered at that such trivial things as the contents of a portmanteau escaped him ?

He was notorious for never knowing what he possessed, or where he left his possessions. He would start out on a journey with a full kit, and return perfectly happy with an empty one.

"Hullo, Hugh ! what have you lost *now ?*"

"Most extraordinary thing," he would reply, quite unconscious of any irony in the question ; "but I can't find my left boot. Here's the right one. Are you sure I didn't leave it in your room ?"

The "strangers' drawer" on the stations in his district, where his visits were always most welcome, invariably contained something he had left behind on a previous trip : a shirt, a pair of socks, a singlet, or a handkerchief. In fact, his failing in this particular line was as well known as the morning breeze, and naturally entailed a considerable amount of chaff.

This he took kindly enough, merely suggesting that if the chaffer were only as blind as he was—for he was very short-sighted—the boot might be on the other foot.

Once, however, an opportunity occurred for retaliation—an opportunity of which he took every advantage, and with the most surprising result ; a result, in short, which has never yet been properly determined, and the key to which he alone possesses. And this was how.

The Session ended, the members speedily dispersed to their respective homes, and Hugh Daventry thankfully found himself on board the good steamer *Kroro-longa*, bound, not for other climes, but for the north, where he lived, and where he could leave off all his clothes if he liked, and they never would be missed.

His cabin mate was Teddy Beade, a most particular chum, and much addicted to pleasantry.

Teddy was an Irishman, clever as they are made, and full of a " right merrie conceit." No one enjoyed a joke more than he did, either at his own or any one else's expense. He preferred the latter of course, and it generally happened that his preference came off. He was seldom worsted in an argument, however abstruse, for if he found himself drifting he would turn on, Dan O'Connell-like, such a roaring cataract of words that his opponent could only feebly gasp under the douche—" What will you have to drink ? "

.   .   .   .   .

The last bell clanged on the steamer's deck with a nerve-jarring clamour ; perspiring stewards rushed through the saloon and round the quarter-deck, screaming, " Any one for the shore ? " and the gangways were choked with visitors hurrying off.

The Captain, in gold-laced cap, suddenly appeared on the wharf-side of the upper bridge and watched the retreating crowd, occasionally nodding or waving his hand to a passing friend.

The last " Goodbye,-dear," and " Don't-forget-to-write" had been said, and the gangways rattled ashore.

" Let go that after-spring ! "   " All clear aft, sir." A ting of the engine-room bell, and an answering plomp from the screw, " Let go forward," and the *Krorolonga* gently sheered off into the stream.

The railings were lined from stem to stern with passengers fluttering farewells, and the wharf looking like a Monday morning drying ground in a gale of wind, responded.

"Well, old chappie," said Teddy to Hugh, "are you quite sure you've got everything? You didn't leave your portmanteau on the wharf, did you? Where are your spectacles?"

Hugh Daventry clutched his coat pockets for an instant in some doubt; then, seeing the laughing face of his friend, he exclaimed—

"Oh, shut up! I'm all right. The steward's got my things, and my spec's are where they ought to be. But, come on out of this crowd, and let's talk over the new ' ad valorem ' duties."

And so the steamer wended her way slowly down the river full speed and across the broad bay at its mouth, and out into the open sea beyond. Here her course was set due north for a thirty hours' run to the first port of call, and the gold-laced Captain descended from his post on the bridge and gave cheery greetings to his passengers.

The sea was smooth and oily. There was no visible horizon to the eastward, nor colour to the water. The blazing, glaring sun seemed to have licked up all, and left only a faint suggestion of skimmed milk.

A long undulating swell occasionally rolled in from the south-east, telling of what had once been a mighty wind, and a pair of porpoise lovers, out for an afternoon stroll, would break the summit with their glistening backs.

Westward, a few handfuls of cotton wool flattened against the sky behind the deep blue coast range, betokened thunderstorms. As night closed in these gave out wondrous lights. A flickering fringe of brilliant and dazzling silver rippled along the edges, and frequent bursts of pink and gold revealed the whole mass in startling and silent beauty.

The passengers had for the most part subsided into deck chairs, or lay sprawling on the up-tilted skylights. The terrible infant had gorged his last banana and bun and was spread out on the deck apoplectically asleep, open-mouthed, and fly-tickled, his mother stooping down at intervals to flick away the aggressive insects the while she stitched at a small red garment.

Odd and disconnected laughter came from the smoking-room in the stern, where four enthusiasts in shirt sleeves were playing "the sort of whist that leaves thumb-marks on the cards," smoking the strongest cigars, and imbibing lemon squashes with a dash.

A faint but everlasting tinkle rose up from the saloon piano, which some school misses had seized upon to display their term's acquirements in the often-encored-by-themselves rendering of the "Dewdrop on the Oyster," and the "Snowflake in the Camp Oven," and all the waltzes they could and couldn't play.

At times a stout, elderly traveller would awake with a snort, and indulge in audible profanity while he shifted his chair farther away from the open skylight through which the music was wafted, and settled himself for another perspiring snooze.

The swish, swish, thump, thump, thump of the screw went rhythmically on, and perhaps there was a certain element of peace around on that sweltering summer's afternoon.

Hugh and Teddy were perfectly happy. They

talked and smoked, and talked till the dinner bell rang, talked through the dinner, and talked till the lights went out suddenly and they found themselves alone on the deck, damp with the heavy dew which had crept in under the awning.

And so to the second night, when their journey would be ended.

Their destination was one of the numerous islands on the coast, under the lee of which a small tender would be in readiness to take off passengers and mails and cargo, and convey them to the town, a few miles up a shallow, sand-shifting river.

The steward was instructed to call them when the tender was ready to start, and they peacefully slumbered. They never heard or felt the stopping of the screw, or the rattle of the anchor-chain, or the slight bump and the scrunching of fenders as the little steamer squeezed alongside in the hot, still hours of the night ; neither did they heed the whisperings as the steward ushered in a new passenger, who promptly coiled himself up in the inside lower bunk and went to sleep.

" The second whistle's gone, gentlemen ! You've got a quarter of an hour."

This was the voice of the steward, and the two friends at once climbed down from their bunks and hurriedly dressed.

Teddy was finished first, and turned as he was leaving the cabin, to say—

" Now, my dear Hugh, be careful, and don't leave any of your belongings behind, and don't forget your spectacles ! "

" You just clear out," said Hugh, and Teddy

disappeared into the alley-way leading to the main deck.

Hugh Daventry cast one last look round the cabin, and his eyes lit on a *pair of boots*. They were not his certainly, as he had got his on. Then they must be Teddy's—Teddy's boots! Hurrah! His opportunity had come at last. Now he would have revenge. Now he would stop that eternal chaff, and Teddy's tongue should be silenced for the whole of ever! What luck!

So, chuckling, he jammed a boot into each pocket of his overcoat, threw it across his arm, grasped his bag and groped his way forward as the last whistle sounded on board the tender.

A few "good-nights," mingled with the jarring of the anchor winch, and the ting ting of the engine bell, and the lights of the big steamer gradually faded away as the little one passed off into the darkness.

Hugh hugged himself over the boots. It was but a poor little joke after all, but it meant a lot to him, and he would make the most of it.

An hour's fussing, an occasional grating of the keel as the little vessel ground her way over a shoal, a loud whistle—a long, two shorts, and a long whistle—and just as the hand of dawn spread a rose-pink film across the eastern sky, the wharf was reached.

Here a few of the early ones who seldom sleep before the pubs. are shut, and never after they are opened, and the hotel waiters who never sleep at all, were assembled with the regular wharf hands, and the tender was made fast.

A few minutes' walk brought the two friends to their

hotel. The street they traversed was thick and soft with dust, with a dark crust of dew lying upon it. A few dogs rose lazily out of the way, leaving white patches where they had slept, and deep footprints as they slowly slunk away; and over all was the warm smell of night in a tropical town.

The room into which they were conducted by the sleepless waiter was full of that warm scent, dished up with kerosine. A faint light still issued from a smouldering lamp, the sticky glass bulb of which was thick with a mass of mosquitoes and midges and moths, and a well-defined rim on the oil-cloth table cover showed how continuous suicides of these pests had been kept up through the night.

"Phew!" said Teddy. "This is a bit sultry! But here we are safe and sound; and now, Hugh, old chap, what have you left behind?"

Hugh was tugging at both his pockets in suppressed excitement, and as the boots were released he rounded on his mate with—

"Now, look here!" and his voice was slow and deliberate. "You are always hammering away at me for losing things, but I've got you at last! Yes, I've got you. *Look at those boots!*"

And he triumphantly banged the boots on the table with such a force that the lamp glasses rattled again, and another blob of mixed midnighters slipped silently off on to the cloth.

"*Look at those boots!*"

Teddy, apparently surprised, did look at them. He picked them up, and turned them over, and put them down again.

"Well," he inquired at last, "what about them?"

“What about them?” almost screamed Hugh. “Why, man, don’t you recognise your own boots?”

Teddy lifted one of his feet and then the other, to make sure he had got any boots on, before replying.

“My boots? Why I never saw them in my life before!”

“Oh, this is too much!” sighed Hugh.

“Too much? What on earth do you mean? Where did you get them?”

“Get them? Just listen to him. Why, in the cabin, of course, after you left.”

“Then, my dear old Hugh,” said Teddy, as solemnly as he could. “They must belong *to the man we left asleep there.*”

“What?” gasped Hugh. “Was there any one else in the cabin?”

“Of course there was! He must have come in off the tender before we were roused up, and turned straight into the lower bunk opposite you.”

“And I never saw him!” said Hugh. “Well, *I am——*”

“Yes, and you well may be, for you are guilty of petty larceny of the meanest and commonest description. It means fourteen days’ at least, without the option of a fine, and how will that be for my right honourable friend, the Minister for——”

“Oh, do shut up,” groaned Hugh. “And let me think.”

Then after a pause—

“I say, Teddy.”

“Well, what is it, my gentle burglar?”

“Look here, old man, you—well, hang it all—you won’t——”

" No," said Teddy deliberately, as he put a hand caressingly on Hugh's shoulder. " No, old chap, I won't ! "

.   .   .   .   .

But what did he do with them ? Exactly ; what *did* he do with them ?

Did he expend much money in telegraphing and forwarding the st—— *lost* boots to their rightful owner, or did he leave them on the table in the company of that smouldering and smelling lamp, and those monumental mounds of kerosined insects ? What would *you* have done with them ?

THE OLD G. P. O.

BY JOHN ELKIN

16   225

THE OLD G. P. O.

BY JOHN ELKIN

"This yellow slave
Will knit and break religions . . .
This is it
That makes the wappen'd widow wed again."
TIMON OF ATHENS.

IT was in the Roaring Fifties! The vast staring bay was dotted thick with dirty-white sails of countless passenger ships, filled to overflowing with the most mixed variety of human cargo. The one absorbing aim of these feverish wanderers—including the sailors before the mast—was to reach that new Land of Ophir, the far-famed "diggings" of Ballarat and Bandigo. Gold, the mightiest of the devil's magicians and agents, had lured them all those thousands of miles across the weary waste of waters, from their poverty-stricken homes and dreary avocations in the overcrowded cities or sleepy villages of the Old Country. Of the eager thousands who week by week entered Port Philip Heads, how many—or how few —would ever reach their fancied Eldorado in that dark, mysterious, unknown, gold-besprinkled bush!

On the southern outskirts of Melbourne, between

river and bay, arose a township of tents, where those
unable to find housing in the city were huddled
together in the blinding sun-glare, and amid indescribable dust and discomfort.   Nor did Canvas Town (as
it was called) suffice.   Many had to lie under the open
sky, at the mercy of fierce suns and pitiless rains.
Delicately nurtured women gave birth to babes
beneath the wind-swept sheds of " Cole's Wharf." The
good ship, *Duke of Bedford*, moored alongside the pier,
was converted into a huge densely-packed boarding
house.   " Delightful Marine Residence," so ran the
alluring legend—" Boatage Found into the Bargain."
It was the Roaring Fifties.   And Melbourne itself
was simply Bedlam.   Men of every race, creed, and
colour hustled one another in its ill-lighted, thronging
thoroughfares.   At night they were packed sardine-
wise in foul, unventilated, dingy rooms ; and the tariff
of squalid Little Bourke Street rivalled the princely
prices of Park Lane or the Old Court suburb.
These feverish souls might roughly be catalogued
under two heads—diggers " down for a spree," or
" new chums " waiting to make their plunge for
Eldorado.
The lucky digger was the reigning monarch—while
his gold-dust lasted !   For him was the world's obei-
sance, and the ready smiles of the consenting fair.
His pinnacle of glory was, as the Napoleon of the
tap-room, to order bottles of champagne at a fabulous
price, to be decanted in tin buckets, from which
monstrous vessels his slavish admirers noisily drank to
the hero's health.   Ah ! what a gloriously free-handed,
open-hearted fellow he was !   And how he literally
emblazoned the female emigrant—erstwhile some

lowly handmaiden or half-starved domestic "help"—
in golden rings and trinkets, and so gorgeously arrayed
her in feathers, flowers, and furbelows, that the river
promenades, where in close embrace they walked
abroad, shone with more than tropic resplendence.
The language, too, of these strange lovers was often
intensely tropical. Such sexual gaiety and emotional
extravagance led sometimes to church—and sometimes not ! Still, the average lucky digger was eccle-
siastically inclined ; and had Gothic cathedrals then
existed in Ophir, he would have scorned to be united
to his flaunting fair in any less magnificent edifice.
Weddings were indeed frequent and promiscuous.
Nor was the " new chum " maiden as a rule at all
backward or bashful. Ancient records reveal the story
of one bouncing Portsmouth lass who went through
the sacred ceremony five several times, with five various
auriferous swains. But perhaps a veil should be drawn
over these wilder doings of the Roaring Fifties. For
such disclosures may not only wound the tender
sensibilities of staid and surviving descendants, but
perchance tend to the upsetting of established inheri-
tances, and proprietary rights.

    .   .   .   .   .

And what a time it was—the Roaring Fifties !
The ancient, overgrown, and extremely unpreten-
tious wooden bungalow which did duty as the General
Post Office (a vastly different structure to the present
palace, but on the same site) has long since been
demolished. But in its day " The Old G. P. O." was
the glory and crown of Melbourne. For years it was
the "address" of a more distinguished, if more mixed

and heterogeneous, shoal of human-kind than almost any club in Christendom. Its low-roofed verandah was the Rialto of early Melbourne.

Old Governor Bourke and his surveyor, who laid out the city, humorously located its "hub" in a deep gully—originally the bed of a flowing creek. This creek had been dammed up, the gully filled with blocks of blue-stone, and converted into the main northern highway to the diggings—and on to Sydney itself. Sir Richard proudly called this great achievement "Elizabeth Street"—not, as is sometimes supposed, in honour of the Tudor queen, but after his own wife; at the same time very properly and conjugally naming the chief intersecting thoroughfare after himself.

And so they boldly stand—BOURKE AND ELIZABETH STREETS—to this day, "to witness if I lie."

Had old Sir Richard and his surveyor treated this flowing creek and deep ravine æsthetically, they might have changed them into an artificial lake or lagoon, a cool and blessed Serpentine, in the midst of that parched and dust-swept city. But those high official utilitarians of the Fifties were all for straight, broad roads, intersecting at right angles, on the approved "chess-board" pattern. Hence arose modern Melbourne—a city "magnificent" to the man of commerce, and to the peripatetic journalist, but distasteful and saddening to the poet and the lover of the picturesque.

Old prehistoric denizens of the original little bush township "before the gold," were wont irreverently to call this famous street of Elizabeth "The Glue-Pot"; and ancient colonial records are full of such preposterous stories as that of the belated traveller who in the pitch blackness of these lampless nights stumbled across a man's hat in the middle of this quagmire of a road. In his anger he would fain have kicked the thing into the open sewers, then muddily flowing like yellow fiends to poison the once pellucid Yarra. But his avenging foot, poised in mid-air, was suddenly arrested by a muffled voice inside the hat exclaiming, "For God's sake, stranger, lift me out. *My horse is underneath.*"

Although Art may outwardly appear all-powerful, even to the extent of transforming things from their original uses, Nature has an awkward habit of unexpectedly re-asserting her sway, and, as it were, of rudely disclosing her primal intention. So, when the fierce tropic rains of that dry and sultry land would come down in torrents, the wide-open gutters of the new Cheapside would suddenly overflow their channels, making the entire roadway into a raging yellow river, which, in its mad fury, would even dash itself, like a thing possessed, against the sacred portals of the Old G. P. O. itself.

'Twas a close sultry morning, that dreaded sirocco, the north wind, blowing shoals of hot dust fiercely along Elizabeth Street, when a young fellow sought shelter under the familiar low-roofed Verandah. Dick Dawlish hardly came under either of the two categories of the Fifties. He was neither a lucky digger nor a new chum. For all his loosely-fitting, slop-made, Scotch tweeds, striped flannel shirt, and broad flapping wide-awake, he was unmistakably a gentleman of the purely English or insular type, with the public school hall-mark stamped indelibly all over him. But if not "colonial," Dick Dawlish was at least "acclimatised."   He had all the air of a fellow who knew his "way about," even in these rough, chaotic times ; and, indeed, he had been at half a dozen "rushes," and dug, none too successfully, ·the golden gullies from Fryer's Creek to Bendigo, and from Ballarat to the Mount.

His bronzed, sunburnt face was bold and even handsome. Fine dark, fearless eyes, good big bridge to the nose, clear-cut, mobile lips, long firmly-curved chin, made up a powerful profile ; while the fine muscular figure and somewhat defiant carriage of the head revealed an almost soldierly bearing. He was at that glorious period of life—five-and-twenty—when the world still has undiscovered regions to dream of or explore.

"I am," said the young man aloud, "as one at the parting of the ways."

And he lounged against the old Verandah post, and knitted his brow, as in a tangled meditation.

Just then there suddenly bobbed round the Little Bourke Street corner a young man who evidently recognised the meditative figure in Scotch tweeds. Any one would have guessed the new-comer to be the merrier and more light-hearted of the twain ; but a really keen-sighted observer would have been tempted to declare him also the more commonplace and superficial. Yet, strange to say, he was actually the second son of an English earl. But Nature—though the most uncompromising of aristocrats—seems to scatter her favours at random, or rather where she lists ; oft-times casting her heaven-born patents of nobility into cottages and workshops, while ignoring for generations those who dwell in palaces and amidst the pomp of life.

The Honourable Philip Worsley was indeed the second and vagabond son of that great steadfast pillar of Church and State, the Right Honourable the Earl of Ventnor. Like many another well-born, restless wanderer, the Hon. Philip found himself in Hobson's Bay, suffering from an acute attack of "gold fever," in the Roaring Fifties. "Phil.," as he was familiarly styled by every man, gentle or simple, who had ever "chummed" with him, was always voted "not half a bad fellow." Nothing ever upset him, and he regarded the varying and sometimes trying incidents of pioneer colonial life (to use his own phrase) as "a rattlin' pantomime." Thus, when he found himself "hard up," and in frequent necessity of calling at the Old G. P. O. for letters in the hope of "remittances from home," he one day discovered that the newly-appointed Postmaster-General (with the full-blown title of Honourable and a salary to match) was the son of a Hampshire baker who formerly provided the Ventnor household with bread. Whereat the Hon. Phil. slapped his legs with joy and exclaimed, "That licks Joey Grimaldi."

Making a trumpet of his sunburnt hands and creeping noiselessly on tip-toe behind the brooding figure in Scotch tweeds, the Hon. Philip let loose a "Coo-ee," calculated to startle a blacks' camp in the remote bush. It was distinctly heard and recognised by Bouncing Bess, the popular barmaid at the "Golden Bush," which famous hostelry stood on the other side of Elizabeth Street, in the direction of the old town cemetery.

Dick Dawlish sprang back as if struck by a stock-whip.

"Good God, Phil.!" he exclaimed, "I might have known it was you. If ever by any chance you get within hail of the pearly gates, that's how you'll call up St. Peter, regardless of his condition of nerves, and without a thought for all the cares and worries of his perplexing billet."

"Why so devilish theological, and so beastly glum this morning?" queried the Hon. Phil., who, like most humourists, hated his jokes to miscarry or fall flat.

"Well, I'm considering whether to take my passage home, or to go off again to the diggings. I'm sick of loafing around Melbourne."

"There's only one way to decide these things," said the Hon. Phil., feeling in his pocket: "the spinning of the merry coinage of the realm."

Whereupon up went a sovereign high into the air.

"*Man* we hump our swags; *Woman* we're off before the mast."

But his companion made no response, and the coin fell and leisurely rolled into the open yellow sewer, from which in some disgust its owner had to fish it out.

"Forgive me, Phil.," said Dawlish with a friendly smile. "I'm a devilish dull dog this morning. So utterly sick of the whole gamble of colonial life, that I don't feel disposed to put my immediate future to the hazard of a toss. But it's like you, old fellow, to offer to accompany me, and not to care a curse which way yellow-boy should point our footsteps."

"Not much," said the Hon. Phil. "Life's a

pantomime, Dick, whether in Pall Mall or Elizabeth Street. But, personally, I'd rather hang on a bit longer here."

"It's this abominable 'hanging-on' that I can't stand," exclaimed Dick. "Somehow you and I, and most of the gentlemen section, never seem to get any forrader, Phil. We've no luck. We turn up at every rush but never strike the colour."

"Oh, well, we grub along somehow, and it ain't half a bad life as long as the storekeepers give us tick—and our 'remittances' drop in occasionally at the Old G. P. O.," added Phil. after an ominous pause.

"But my dear Phil., you don't seem to see we're *in* the colony and not *of* it. Besides, things are changing. This Bedlamite business will soon be over, and other people are settling down to something definite, to some fixed social position, or decent calling, while you and I, and poor Steve Dugdale—are all three on the high road to Loaferdom."

"It all comes," said the Hon. Phil., philosophically, "of our ungodly, extravagant bringing-up. It's the fault of our parents. We can rough it with any gipsy tinker of the lot—but we can't save a red cent, and as a rule we've no luck. Would to God I'd been born a hungry German turnip-prodder, or a lantern-jawed Scotch crofter—even a T'othersider. They're the chaps to grub along into millionaires in a country like this."

"Our greatest curse," said Dick Dawlish impressively, "comes in the shape of monetary assistance from our relations at home. It makes us a byeword. Even your friend Bouncing Bess calls us 'R.M.'s.' —Remittance men. It's damned disgusting."

"So it is when the expected coin doesn't turn up, dear boy," said the Hon Phil. "Which reminds me that my Calvinistic aunt, the Lady Letitia, seems to be getting the upper hand again in the Ventnor family. She agrees with you, and thinks these remittances sap our self-reliance. But my manly pride can stand any amount of bank drafts. She don't know how tough my moral fibre is. I'll drop on her yet with an account of my Sunday-school class, and the work I'm doing among the heathen." And the incorrigible young aristocrat winked at the newly-imported Irish policeman, who was listening to this little confidential colloquy with an amused grin on his fine open Hibernian countenance.

How much longer these two young gentlemen would have discussed the colony and their own future prospects, it is impossible to say. But their talk was suddenly interrupted by the most penetrating noise in the world—a street Arab's shrill cry—

The Mail!   English Mail!   Arrival of the Mail!

And soon was heard the scramble and scurrying of hundreds of feet and the hoarse myriad murmurs, mounting to a prolonged roar, of wildly excited men, rushing down from Flagstaff Hill, where they had seen the long-wished-for signals of the mailship's arrival in the bay.

For all this was in the far-off days, which, though but forty years ago, seem like an ancient, dim-recorded, half-forgotten myth—the days before steamships and telegraph cables were known, or even dreamed of, at the Antipodes. Then, indeed, the coming in of the

English mail—conveyed by slow sailing ships in from seventy to one hundred days—with all the wonderful accumulated budget of news, was an event—an epoch —no longer to be realised by the young up-to-date generation of 1899. Let us not, however, in our pride in the achievements of modern science, altogether despise our colonial forefathers. The men of the Roaring Fifties had their compensation for being thus plunged for some three dark months in utter ignorance of the outer world ; theirs was the keen excitement of surprise, the eternal magic of the unexpected ; the edge of novelty was not then blunted by the irritating driblets of the daily cablegrams, and the slow old mail boats brought ample budgets which had all the freshness of sensational news, combined with the fulness of historical records.

It was the fierce, exciting, anxious time of the Crimean War. Fancy those vagabond Britons and wandering gold-diggers rushing down from Flagstaff Hill, in utter ignorance of the fortunes of the great struggle in which the dear old motherland was plunged, and knowing not whether their own un-protected shores were altogether safe from Russian cruisers.

How they surged round the newspaper offices, and wildly rushed down towards the Old G. P. O., breath-less for news from home. What an uproar and stampede ! Above all pierced the shrill cries of the street Arabs—

The Mail !   Arrival of the English Mail !   Full Account of the Rooshian War !   Home News ! One Shilling !

One shilling indeed.   Crowns and half-crowns were tendered with no thought of change for these exciting news sheets.

It had been a sullen, sultry morning, hot and dusty, the sky overhead gleamed like burnished brass.   But low down on the horizon hung those small, floating, everspreading cloudlets, which often seem to grow and gather as one gazes ; and in a short while cover the face of the heavens like a pall, portending sudden change and fierce storm.   Soon huge drops of rain began to fall one by one on the parched and dusty street.

"Ivry dhrop," remarked Connolly, the new Dublin policeman, "hittin' yer wid a wilt loike a five-shullun pace."

But no one minded the coming storm.   The excited crowd grew thick and thicker, and hurled itself against the old Verandah.   Every man was eager for news of the war, and anxious for his home letters.   It was a strange, indescribable Babel.   Still, over all the roar and hubbub broke the street Arabs' shrill cries—

Argus !   'Strornary !   Home News !   Charge of the Light Brigade !   Argus 'Strornary !   Home News ! A Shilling !

Men, and women too, dashed wildly across the widening yellow sewers into the wet road-way, to secure at any price this long pent-up budget or English news.

As these gold-seeking exiles tore open the papers and read of the famous Balaclava charge, hats were waved in the air, and Elizabeth Street was rent with mad, vociferous cheers.

"My God," said Dick Dawlish, "I should like to have been in it."

The rain began to come down faster and fiercer ; it was a thorough tropical flood. But still the excited crowd surged across the wide and almost impassable gutters, into the slushy street for the papers, while the street Arabs, drenched to the skin, yelled more piercingly than ever—

Arrival of the Mail! Argus! Home News! Defeat of the Rooshians! All the News of the War!

For a while people even forgot that they could get their private letters addressed—as so many thousands were at that time—"G. P. O., Melbourne." Even the Hon. Phil. had become for the moment oblivious of the fell designs of the pious Lady Letitia. However, after a while there was a fresh rush in the direction of the Inquiry Window, while the historic Old G. P. O. might well have been mistaken for Drury Lane on boxing night.

A thin, delicate, refined-looking young fellow passed by, just as Dick Dawlish and the Hon. Phil. were making for the window.

"Hullo, Stephen," cried Dick Dawlish. "Glad to see you. Hope you feel better. Isn't the news from the Crimea glorious ? "

With a faint smile and a nod, Stephen Dugdale slipped by them and managed to reach the window, where the clerk handed him his letters.

"What a crush," said the Hon. Phil. "Why,

there's the gay old fossils whose portraits figure in half a dozen of Aunt Letitia's story books. How very odd."

"Ominous, I should call it," said Dick.   "Who are they ? "

" Don't know ; somethin' in the Sunday-school line, or else the scribblin' and poetic business," replied his careless companion.   " These Ballarat nuggets have brought some rum fish over here, Richard."

Had the Hon. Phil. possessed the curiosity to step up behind the comely, pleasant-faced lady and gentleman, as they asked for their letters at the window he might have heard in soft Quaker tones, the query—

" Any letters for William or Mary Howitt ? "

But if the Hon. Phil. was too heedless to identify this remarkable pair of Quaker exiles, a young fellow with a very marked face, who was pressing towards the Inquiry Window evidently recognised them, and was accosted by " William and Mary."

" Why," said the lady with delight, " if it isn't young Mr. Wordsworth.   It seems but yesterday since I saw thy dear grandfather ? "

This historic little group of English exiles, attracted no attention whatever from the surging crowd round the window. They were soon joined by a young digger whom Dick Dawlish evidently knew. For he shouted out, "Hullo Woolner! How's the plaster-cast business getting on ? "   And in truth, speaking to the grandson of the great English poet, was the future pre-Raphaelite and Royal Academician.   Yes ! there were some strange groups under the Old G. P. O. Verandah in the Roaring Fifties on " mail day."

No sooner had young Mr. Wordsworth and Thomas Woolner got their letters and hurried off than the Hon. Phil.'s attention was again arrested by the entrance of a tall, spare, dark-haired, heavy-browed, "aloof-looking" young gentleman, who looked the tourist more than the digger.

"Why," exclaimed Phil, "I'm blowed if it ain't a friend of the governor's. Don't want him to spot me."

And he stepped into the darkest corner of the Verandah and hid himself behind Dawlish.

"Looks rather a masterful chap," said Dick, eying the stranger at the window.

This chance remark was not altogether a bad shot ; for the young gentleman so lightly referred to was destined to become, more than once, "Master" of the British Empire.

But if none of those native exiles with historic names made the least stir as they jostled in the crowd of the Old G. P. O. Verandah, this was not the case with a black-browed, sallow-faced man who now entered, clamping his spurs on the weather-board floor, and leaning his hand heavily on a pistol in his belt. Everybody made way for this great personage, while an expansive smile of heart-felt joy spread over the jocund countenance of the Hon. Phil., who nudged his moody companion.

"Don't miss him, Dick. It's worth a king's ransom to see Cornelius O'Regan call for his mail letters."

It was, indeed, the great Irish tragedian, whose sonorous tones had thrilled the lovers of Shakespeare and the "legitimate," and whose name was indeed a household word to the stage-struck shop-boys of Drury Lane as well as to the perspiring diggers of the old Charlie Napier at Ballarat. A hero indeed! The great Cornelius inquired for his correspondence in a voice like that of Hamlet's ghostly father, audible to the entire audience under the old Verandah, and even penetrating into the recesses of the bungalow so as to thrill the very souls of the over-worked clerks of the Old G. P. O.

"There were four different ladies last mail day," said the clerk at the window, "each demanding letters addressed to Mrs. Cornelius O'Regan. To whom am I to deliver them?"

Ah! then it was a noble spectacle to see the great impersonator of Othello and Belphegor (the mountebank) smite his mighty brow and exclaim—

"*Four!*—did you say *four*, varlet? Nay, this cannot be! And I a man of pure and stainless life!"

Then, without deigning further to parley with the official, the great man stalked majestically away, muttering in a stage whisper, plainly audible within the recesses of the building itself—

> " Be thou as chaste as ice, as pure as snow,
> Thou shalt not escape CALUMNY!"

And he threw such weird emphasis on the word "CALUMNY" that it sounded as some old Arabian charm—an unfamiliar thing of beauty and mystery— like unto that dear old word "Mesopotamia!" With bowed head, the great tragedian passed into the dripping streets and slowly clanked out of sight, the picture of a mighty soul in trouble — an injured angel in a naughty world !

"By heavens!" exclaimed the Hon. Phil., "that's too gorgeous! It means quite fifty quid in the dress-circle to-night at the old 'Iron Pot.'"

"Fifty quid in the old 'Iron Pot?'" queried the puzzled Dick. "What the devil do you mean?"

"Why, that's Cornelius O'Regan, and he's playing at the Olympic—the old iron theatre, you know, at the top of Lonsdale Street. It's a little 'ad.,' a put-up job. Don't you tumble to it? He's given the josser at the window half a dozen seats to ask him that question about the four Mrs. Corneliuses. So that he could throw the 'Calumny' speech off his chest when the blessed old Verandah was packed on mail day! It's magnificent, and worth *quite* fifty quid in the house to-night. Oh! I'm up to the whole bag of tricks, Richard."

But the Hon. Phil. did not think it necessary to tell his friend that he himself had once assisted in a similar little dramatic scene when "business" was rather slack at the old Charlie Napier at Ballarat (where he was then going on nightly as a "super") ; and how the old Eureka diggers rushed the theatre that night, and threw their nuggets at the feet of the virtuous tragedian.

The Hon. Phil. at last squeezed in front of the "Inquiry Window." When, in reply to his eager question, the clerk curtly replied, "Nothing"; he cheerfully nodded, and remarked, to the amazement of that harassed but versatile official—

"Many thanks, old son. Thought as much. As I expected, Letitia's got the upper hand. Good day ; see you at the 'Iron Pot' to-night."

Dick Dawlish's turn came ; and he too had no home letters.

When the two young men attempted to pass out from under the old Verandah, they saw that the Elizabeth Street gutters had invaded the side-walk and were running frantically half across the wide roadway itself. The rain continued to come down in torrents. The rushing waters were quite impassable, even by the arched footbridges at the street corners. Men and women were being conveyed across the flooded street in carts at half-a-crown a head.

A sudden noisy splash ! A man had stumbled and fallen into the midst of this madly-flowing, dangerous yellow torrent. Dick Dawlish, fleet and sure of foot as a reindeer, rushed wildly through the shallow water of the pathway, and springing with a bound on to the centre of the footbridge, swooped down and caught the drifting figure just as it was being sucked through the narrow arch. " Hold on to the sides," he shouted ; and then with a powerful jerk drew poor Stephen Dugdale out of the perilous floodtide, and landed him on the narrow footbridge—a spectacle indeed for gods and men !

" Did yez see *that?*" yelled the delighted Connolly, the Irish constable. " The grip he tuk av his back-bone ! Begorra, but he'd be an ornimint to the foorce."

" 'The week afore last," said a man, by way of comment, " a little fat cove fell in, and was jammed to death under that there very bridge. I seed them haul him out like a drownded rat."

" But he was only a blasted Frenchman," remarked a big rough-looking bushman, burnt to a brick. "Wot can you expect? Them foreigners, they ain't got the gumption to clutch on to the bridge, and haul theirselves out."

Despite the fact that the French were then our "allies," the colonial Briton regarded foreigners and Frenchmen as synonymous — and inferiors. The spirit of Horatio Nelson still held sway.

Such "street incidents" were not at all uncommon in the Fifties. And a foreign tourist had actually been drowned in this manner, in the old Elizabeth Street gutter, at flood time.

"Come along, Dick," exclaimed the ever-cheerful Phil. "Let us take poor Steve over to the 'Golden Bush' and get Bessie to hang him up to dry."

AN AUSTRALIAN ROSE

BY MRS. PATCHETT MARTIN

AN AUSTRALIAN ROSE

BY MRS. PATCHETT MARTIN

TO R. M. P.

TO her of gracious gifts, whose graceful pen
    Becomes a fairy wand in her frail hand,
    Flashing the sunlight of her Austral land
On the slim maidens and brown-bearded men
    Who live their lives for us at her command,
I said — "I always think of you as when,
Like one entranced in an enchanted glen,
    You stood one night amidst a madcap band.

With red lips parted, and a roseleaf flush
    Painting the pearly pallor of your face,
Mute, motionless, in an expectant hush,
    Your dreamy eyes like stars shone into space."
Softly she answer'd with a shadowy blush—
    "My soul first stirred to life in that fair
        place!"

THE SLEEPING SICKNESS OF LUI THE KANAKA

BY LALA FISHER

THE SLEEPING SICKNESS OF LUI
THE KANAKA

BY LALA FISHER

"PLEASE, Mr. Wilton," said my overseer, appearing suddenly at the door of the dining-room one sunny morning at seven o'clock, "there's worse news than ever."

"Well, Elgar," I answered, without excitement, carrying a piece of well-buttered toast to my mouth, "what's up now?"

"Wopobra is down! I missed him at his breakfast, and on going to his hut found him lying asleep on his bunk, with his face to the wall; and there he'll lie till he dies and rots, if we'll let him."

I rose, pushing back my chair so hurriedly that it toppled over, and taking a quick turn up and down the room, thought bitterly of the aspect of success in store for the sugar industry over whose interests I was paid to watch. Only last month I had to send three Kanakas into the township suffering with leprosy, and now the Kanakas were dying at the rate of eight for the past three weeks. One, the first, died of dengue fever. There was no mistake about *that*; but his successor had no sign of fever nor illness of any sort. He just made up his mind to die, turned his face to the wall, and in two days was dead. So with a third " boy," then a fourth, another, and another, until I was fairly puzzled. Johnny, a stalwart, broad-shouldered, and healthy " boy," took to his bunk one fine morning, and neither the pokes of Elgar nor the curses of the black overseer of his gang had the slightest effect in rousing him. He, too, pegged out, and had been buried last night.

Elgar's news worried me horribly. Wopobra was one of the most reliable and honest workers on the plantation—a heavy, knock-kneed " Tanna " boy, with the laughing mouth, perfect teeth, and wondering eyes of his countrymen. He had been fifteen years on the place, and now superintended the cane-cutting of a large gang of new " boys."

Presently I took my hat down from the peg on the door, left my scarcely-opened egg, swallowed the contents of my coffee cup, and followed Elgar down the yard and across the space to the boys' huts. We soon reached the one of which we were in search, and lifting up the heavy bag hanging across the door, I entered.

Wopobra was, as Elgar had said, lying absolutely motionless, with a blanket over his shoulder, and his face hidden next the wall. The outlines of his high hip, clumsy feet, and one sprawling hand, with the delicate and filbert-nailed fingers peculiar to his race, gave me the impression of a man—to use a common term—" throwing up the sponge." For all the sign of life he gave he might have been already dead. I crossed over and gave his curly head a pull. " Well, Wopobra, what sort of game you call this, eh ?" A moan was the only answer. "Here, get up," I said, giving him a more vigorous pull, " get up and do your work. What for you skulk, you lazy hound ? Get up," and yet a third pull.

I might as well have tugged at a corpse.

"Perhaps he's dead," Elgar suggested, and I bent over his face.

" Dead, not he—shamming more likely," and with Elgar's help I caught him by the shoulders and got him into a sitting position.

"You lazy dog," I said angrily, "lift yourself up," hoping to arouse him by rough words, calm ones having had not the faintest effect with the other boys now dead.

He opened his eyes and looked into my face so dully and stupidly, that I felt half a pang at the mode of treatment I had adopted, but I determined to give it yet a few more minutes' trial, for, truth to tell, I was in despair about these easy-dying chaps. Shaking, kicking, swearing, proved not of any avail however ; directly it was over he fell back in an inert heap, and so we left him.

On our way to the mill I called at the hut of the native doctor of the herd. Lui was inside—his work hours did not commence until nine, as he was not overstrong, and so was allowed the easy billet of throwing the stacks of cane upon the feeders. " Go down to Wopobra—he plenty ill," I said. " Suppose you make him well, I give you £1, Lui."

Lui spread out his hands and rolled his eyes. " No good, boss," he droned dolefully, " He die soon—he *feel* him gwine to die—he no try live now." As he spoke a thought flashed through my mind, and I retraced my steps to Wopobra's bedside.

It was too late ; the poor wretch was dead !

That night I sat hour after hour in my squatter chair on the moonlit verandah, and smoked pipe after pipe as I endeavoured to arrive at some satisfactory solution of these extraordinary deaths.

First and foremost I came to the conclusion that a great deal of it had to do with the Kanakas' well-known habit of "caving in." Any planter who employs boys (and who does not ?) will tell you that sometimes if his fingers ache, one of these men will lie down and die ; a fit of biliousness, a short bout of toothache, and he will neither eat nor be comforted. If the fit takes him, he quietly dies.

Secondly, I concluded that if some drastic measure could dispel the lethargy through which the lazy fellow found so comfortable an egress from the world, a cure might possibly be effected. Plan after plan occurred to and was rejected by me, until at last I hit upon one that I thought might suit my purpose. Just as the glorious Queensland morning light was glimmering rosily over the cane tops—my usual hour for rising, I went in and tumbled on the bed, boots and all, for a short rest before breakfast.

That morning passed without any unusual incident. Wopobra was buried at sunrise, and towards evening his comrades gathered together, after they had knocked off work, to watch the burning of his hut and its contents. I turned to leave when this was done. "Where is Lui ? " I asked. I required him to take a turn at rolling my tennis lawn, but I could not distinguish his face among the crowd.

" Here, Sammy," and I beckoned to a mate of his.
" Go and find Lui, and help him to roll the lawn."

Sammy tramped off to find him, and I walked slowly
up to the house, thinking no more of the matter.

After perhaps the lapse of half an hour, the house-
keeper's .knock woke me out of a nodding doze, and
she informed me that Sammy would like to speak to
me. I went out slipperless to the back verandah steps.
" Well, Sammy ? "

" Please, boss, Lui plenty sick ! "

" What ! " I almost yelled ; " say it again, you
black devil ; *what !* "

" Lui, he die soon," Sammy said stolidly. " Lui, he
plenty sick ! "

" Oh, indeed ! " and I laughed sarcastically. "We'll
soon see to that. Sick is he ? He'll be sick before I've
finished with him."

My patience, never my strongest point, had at last
given way, and I went inside and laced up my boots
with a grim determination in my heart to knock the *die*
out of my friend Lui. I took down a heavy stockwhip
from its nail on the verandah ; and so great was my
indignation, and so unmeasured my haste, that in
hurrying from the house I slipped down the last eight
steps and nearly broke my neck. At boiling point I
hastened past the mill and the clumps of huts, grasping
yet tighter the coiled stockwhip in my hand, until I
reached Lui's abode. Then my whip sprang out as
if by magic. I whirled it round my head with a
resounding crack. "Here, Lui," I yelled, " come out
of that."

No answer—a silence like the grave.

" Lui, you black devil " ; and I made his walls shake

where the whip whistled about them. "Come here,
I say, or I'll hide the liver out of you."

A rustle inside and Lui appeared, but sunk in a
heap at the door, even as his hand parted the bags.
"Me welly bad, boss," he whined; "me soon
die!"

"Die, be damned," I said grimly." "I'll die you."
I squeezed behind him and planted in the middle of
his bent back a kick that sent him well out in the
front of the house. Then I prodded him with the
butt end of the whip. "Get up and RUN, Lui," I
said insinuatingly. "I'LL make you well—run—run—
RUN, you ebony hell-cat, RUN." Each word I empha-
sised with a flick from the whip-end. Soon he dimly
realised the necessity for rising and immediate flight,
and he crept to his hands and knees and turned on me
so pitiful a gaze, with his mouth working and his
frame shaking, that I almost faltered in my purpose
—ALMOST, not quite.

"You pig-dog—hell-beast," I shrieked, "GET UP
AND RUN," and I brought the whip heavily round his
flanks. As it curled above my head for a second
blow, *he did run;* my God! HOW HE RAN! The
cracker of my whip just tickled his moleskin clad calf,
and he was off like a deer. Down one of the paths
between the cane he flew, and I followed. I couldn't
get at him in the cane, *there* the whip was useless to
me, but soon he reached the end of that short patch
and ran into the bullock-yard, screaming like a badly-
pithed ox.

Ah, ha! I had him now.

He attempted time after time to clamber up the
slabs and over the fence, but I flicked a bit of his skin

every time, so savagely that he could not reach the top, and fell headlong to the ground.

Round and round that bullock-yard I lashed him —lashed his Crimean shirt to ribbons—lashed great weals upon his chest and shoulders and across his arms, until at length my arm refused further service, and fell helpless at my side. His shrieks for mercy stopped, and he stood for an instant silent and at bay, with fiery, hunted eyes and labouring chest. The veins in his throat stood out like cables, and his hands clenched and unclenched themselves in an agony of feeling. Then, when he realised that the whip had fallen he rushed over and feel on his knees before me.

" Boss, boss," he groaned harshly and brokenly, and a flood of tears poured from his bloodshot eyes ; " Boss, boss, I will no die ! I will no die."

I just leant against the rails and looked at him— too exhausted to speak. I noticed his exquisitely-shaped hands, hands over which a painter would have raved ; *how* he wrung them, *how* he sobbed, cringing in the dirt before me like a cruelly chastised child.

After some moments I put out my hand and let it sink into the mass of curls running over his head.

" You get well, Lui," I panted, " or I'm damned if I don't do it again."

Slowly and with effort I passed the whip from my stiff and blistered fingers into my left hand, and leaving Lui abjectly grovelling in the dust of the yard, I went on my way to the house.

THERE WERE NO MORE DEATHS.

THE OLD SCENES

A SKETCH

BY MRS. CAMPBELL PRAED

THE OLD SCENES

A SKETCH

BY MRS. CAMPBELL PRAED

"IS that all?" said a pretty sick girl on our steamer, who had had her chair brought close to the bulwarks, that she might not miss the first sight of Sydney Harbour. "Oh, I don't call it much more than just pretty. Seems somehow as if the mountains had been forgotten."

She expressed it exactly. One does feel as if the Creator had forgotten the mountains. And yet, indeed, how beautiful Sydney Harbour is, though one begins to wonder whether it is as beautiful as the harbour of Nagasaki, or of Hong Kong, or even of Algiers, or of many other places one has heard less about. There is always the want of the background.

Strangely enough, I didn't seem to be steaming gently into Sydney Harbour in this big Orient boat, on this summer afternoon, but to have gone back— oh, ever so many years—to a certain wild morning, when the sea was all grey and dirty-white, heaving and growling after a great storm, in which a little brig—she was called *The Briton's Queen* I remember —had gallantly held her own, though the English mail steamer was in peril of her life, and more than one ship went down off the coast that night. Brave little *Briton's Queen !* I can scent now in my nostrils the briny freshness of that squally morning, and oh, the delight of it after a day and a night with hatches down in a cabin half full of water, and a smell—an unforgetable and intolerable smell — of decaying apples. *The Briton's Queen* was freighted with fruit, and we had been a fortnight in making the voyage from Tasmania. Nothing of that voyage remains in my memory but the smell of the apples, the gale, and the feeling of intense exhilaration, as our little ship, with her sails set, scudded over the waves on that tempestuous morning and passed between Sydney Heads into balmy peace.

There it was again—the break in the grey-blue line of cliff, the two huge profiles of rock—the boldest with a lighthouse upon it, and the ocean roaring against its iron rampart. A little boat with a reddish sail raced the big steamer round the North Head and won the race. And now we were in perfectly smooth water, a blue basin with sandy-beached bays curving in and out, and a flotilla of boats—it was Saturday afternoon—dancing about the points.

There flashed into my memory another entry into Sydney Harbour—this a night one—after a second voyage from Tasmania ; and the thrill of hearing out of the darkness, as a boat pulled up to the steamer, the news that the Duke of Edinburgh had been shot by Farrell, the Fenian. Then, next day, the mingled excitement and horror of seeing Sydney placarded with posters offering "£1,000 reward for the accomplices of Farrell."

.   .   .   .   .

It is all confusing, terribly confusing; and the two lightning streaks of impressions are dead trees and hats. Were there always so many dead trees, and did Australians always wear such a bewildering variety of hats?

There are hard felt and soft felt, broad-brimmed and narrow-brimmed, sailor, Panama, Buffalo Bill, Jim Crow, cowboy, and cavalier; hats puggareed, hats bare, and even the white "Derby" chimney-pots. It is a nightmare of hats.

And the dead trees! They, too, have become half a nightmare, half a fascination. These are not the few scattered clumps of "rung" gums, which used to show here and there round a head-station or stockman's hut, in picturesque contrast with the mass of grey-green foliage. All along the railway line there are miles and miles, paddocks full, whole tracts of these livid corpses of trees, which stand bolt upright, stretching forth long naked arms, that twist up and down and interlace each other in weirdly human fashion. At first their deadness seems a mystery, and then one remembers that it is the Free Selector now and not the Squatter who rules the land; and that because of him is its greyness. For it is all grey, all the same dull, dead monotony of colouring—grey two-railed fences, brown-grey grass, green-grey leaves—where there are leaves — yellow-grey sawn-wood houses; grey shingles, grey skeletons, grey ashes, where the skeletons have been burned and the soil made ready for crops of corn and vines and millet and cotton, and all the other good things which the Selector eventually produces. But it takes a long time first to dispossess the gum-trees, which are the inheritors of the ground.

Oh the heat and glare of that railway journey between the skeleton-trees and the two-railed fences! Only here and there, a little township of weather-board houses, bare and straight, with oblongs of windows, like the houses in toy boxes, and their zinc roofs blazing piteously in the scorching sun. It is a relief to see near the townships, beyond the aggressive newness of their stores and public-houses, some sur-vival of an old slab-and-bark homestead, with its patch of pumpkin vines and a few willows and mulberries, and perhaps an orange-tree. That is on the higher land, near the border, where the air has cooled a little.

Here, in a certain region, the skeletons give place to queer grey boulders—everything is always grey—scattered anyhow, in shape of crouching beasts and altar-stones, and fat monoliths. Now, as we descend, steamy rain falls, and the heat is a clammy misery and a prickly aggravation. Night comes. At the different wayside stations friendly hands are stretched forth, and there's a ghostly feeling in the sight of familiar-strange faces—the faces of children grown to manhood and womanhood, and of the middle-aged become old and grey-haired. It is midnight, when at last the thirty hours' train journey is over, and I step into the clammy stove-house atmosphere, and know that, after twenty years, I am once again in mine own land, amidst mine own people.

.   .   .   .   .

Familiar-strange, too, those bush boys on unkempt

bush horses, and with the real bush seat, an easy, slouching oneness with the beast beneath, who are waiting in a clearing of the scrub for the mail to be thrown out as the train passes.

Where are the old landmarks ? Twenty years ago it took a good three days getting from the township to Murrum, and extra horses had to be sent along to pull the buggy through Doondin Scrub. Now it is a question of being three or four hours in a railway carriage, and of a fifteen-mile drive over the range. But how much more exciting it used to be ! The plunge into the gloom of the scrub, the toiling on foot down leafy gullies and up steep muddy pinches, the jibbing of the horses, the shoutings of the black-boys, and all the buggy-breakings and mendings, and the uncertainty as to ultimate possibilities ! Very little remains of the scrub, only a few belts of glossy green, and some of the old bottle trees, which are like historic monuments of some strange order of architecture. So that one might fancy Lemurian builders had raised pillars of a grotesque topsy-turvi-ness, with bulging middle, base tapering inwards and over-loaded capitals. All the way are Selectors' homesteads, set in gardens and orangeries, and where once was dense forest, homely German settlements with school-houses, stores, and plantations of maize, cotton, arrowroot, and even tobacco.

The Selectors in these parts have long passed the skeleton and grey stage ; and all over the hills and on the plains where the scrub used to be, are vivid patches of green and yellow and the red-brown of millet. The clearing of the forest has brought the mountains into view, and it is such a satisfaction to find that years have not dwarfed their outlines, nor imagination magnified their beauty. They are all just as memory painted them—tiers of blue peaks—the border range in the far distance, and the Jerra Crag, with its encircling precipice and turret top, rising between the Murrum hump and twin-peaked Kumbal—as real and good to look at as the Southern Cross and many other things that were of old.

There is with us a little English artist girl, who has lived all her life in London, and an English boy called Rothwell, going to do "colonial experience" at Murrum. The three "M's," Meg (that is the English girl), Marge, and Mena, make as charming a nosegay of maids as could be seen. And there is Cousin William, outrider to the buggy just then, a miner by profession, and self-appointed instructor-general to Meg on things Australian. And there are Terry, Fulvia, and the doctor.

"He's a young one," Terry said, apologetically, as the near horse shied at a stump and tilted Meg almost into the Flagstone Creek. "Only tackled this summer. Never had a better puller. . . . But this won't do. Must attend to my business and not talk. Look out! Here we are coming to a bit of corduroy."

And we found out that "corduroy" meant a road made of little gum trees, and that it jolted exceedingly.

Two men with their blankets rolled into swags were boiling their billy of tea in a gully by the road-side.

"They're humping bluey," explained Cousin William.

"What does that mean?" asked the artist girl,

" They're on the Wallabi track," further explained Cousin William.

Meg asked no more, but later on she made a sketch of " Humping Bluey."

Meg has the air of one to whom no surprising experience can now be a novelty. She has been given tea for breakfast, luncheon, and dinner, at five o'clock and also at eleven a.m. A monstrous frog stared at her out of her washing basin this morning, and she was shown a corrugated black fellow in a ragged shirt and abbreviated trousers, with a brass plate—symbol of sovereignty—on his tattooed breast, and told that he is a king.

We stopped on the shoulder of the dividing range— not the great Border range, but a little one between Cuchin and Murrum. Below stretched the Cuchin plain with its water hole, the Crag beyond, and the head station on a green promontory jutting out into the sea of tall grey-green grass. Now it is "eucalyptic cloisterdom" once more; and we seem as we descend, to be passing through interminable aisles of red-gum trunks and fret work of bough. Locusts whirr intermittently. Never was such rich grass as grows in the furrows of the hills. Meg takes her revenge on Cousin William by drawing his attention to the fine blot of colour which a herd of red cattle make on the grey-green. She wishes him to understand that if he can talk Australese, she can talk Art jargon !

Some of the gums have grotesque protuberances— these are what the shepherds and stockmen used to make *coolimans* out of in the old Bush days; and there are grass trees with spears and tufts, and great brown ant-heaps like queer shaped tombstones.

Then comes a splash through the river at Cuchin crossing, which is close by Murrum stockyard ; and —is it the cornshed of memories ? . . . The paddock is clearer than it used to be, and the river fringe of ti-tree and she-oak has been broken, and there's a grand new Selector's homestead that was not there long ago. The dogs run out barking, Fulvia, young Marge, and Mena, and the St. Bernard, and the cockatoo are at the garden fence—how the lagerstromia and the creepers have grown !—and three peacocks give screeches from the roof of the kitchen gangway. They are moulting, poor things, and terribly ashamed of their draggled tails, but a sense of family obligation and of the dignity of the occasion does not permit them to retire altogether as, for the next week or so, they consistently do.

It is a funny little cluster of wooden cottages Murrum head station, joined together by gangways which are covered with bongainvillea, bignonia, rinkasporum and ever so many other creepers. There are bowery nooks between the verandahs filled in with plants set in stumps and with stag-horn and bird's nest ferns growing upon walls and posts. Here Mena makes a pretty picture in the mornings, learning her lessons, with the St. Bernard panting in the heat at her feet. Inside, the walls are of cedar—it isn't the old drawing-room, but a new room altogether, with windows at the end giving peeps of the Jerra Crag, and the Kumbal peaks, and showing the old mandarin orange tree and quince orchard and the prickly pear hedge. Outside there is a verandah like the deck of a ship, where everybody lounges in cane chairs and the hammock, and eats grapes and water melons, and where we spend the long hot evenings looking on the dim semicircle of mountains and watching the Southern Cross mount from behind Mount Murrum.

.   .   .   .   .

Alas! It is the time of the rains, and for five days and nights the heavens have poured forth water. A blanket of steam has covered the mountains. The air is a vaporous oppression, and over all broods a clammy stillness, broken by the crashing downpour upon a zinc roof, and the spattering upon the window-panes and rebound upon the floor of the verandah. Mena's bower is no longer inviting. The ground is strewn with sodden bongainvillea petals, and the fern tongues drop wetness. The grey stumps in which a little while ago colcas and calladium plants flourished joyously, are now black with moisture, and all the slender stalks are bowed and the downy leaves torn to shreds and drooping and flabby. Mena's magpie is taking a bath in one of the stumps. Now he perches on the hedge, spluttering and spreading his wings with his head cocked on one side, and a wicked look in his little eyes. The Galah parrot toddles up and down disconsolately. There is a soft swish of rivulets blending with the hushed murmur of insects. At night, the frogs and crickets are deafening and the roar of the river grows deeper.

The nasty creeping things come out. A fat tarantula crawls up the curtains, and there's a hundred-legged spider between Meg's blankets; and ants run about in myriads, and get into the jam and sugar, and drop their wings uncannily on the tablecloth. We have no joy now in the verandah, though we draw the cane chairs close to the wall to avoid driving drops, and the doctor and the man from the next station and Cousin William tell grim stories of the bush. The fruit is sodden ; the beast which has been killed has gone bad ; the wood is too damp to burn in the kitchen. Fulvia enters tragically, in her arms a bundle of fine damask, black with mildew, and a snake is killed in the bush house.

That evening the doctor, the man from the next station, and Cousin William tell snake stories, and Meg dreams evil dreams.

The man from the next station has only nine fingers. When he was a little boy, he and his brother went out into the bush with their tomahawks to play at finding 'possums. As he moved a bit of dead wood a black snake bit his forefinger. The man from the next station put his finger straight out on a stump, and told his brother to chop it off, low down, with the tomahawk that very moment. The boy chopped, and then they sucked the wound, and that's how he comes to have only nine fingers.

The doctor too had his snake experience. One night he camped in a newly-built but deserted hut. A sheet of bark was on the ground, he spread his blanket over it and laid him down to sleep. Several times during the night he fancied that the bark heaved beneath him, but he was too tired to take any serious notice. In the morning when he had rolled up his blanket again, he kicked away the piece of bark and saw a great black snake coiled under it.

Cousin William knows a man on the diggings whose nerve broke after the gruesome adventure of one night. The man was travelling alone, and that evening he had camped in the open under a gum tree.

It was bright moonlight. Suddenly, in the very small hours he awoke, feeling something moving over his chest—he was lying on his back barely covered with his blanket, for the night was hot. As he awoke, he saw that a brown snake had coiled itself upon his chest. Now, a brown snake is deadly; and the man had no brandy nor ammonia, nor anything which would save him if he were bitten. For long hours he lay watching. He dared not move, he scarcely dared to breathe. He nursed the loathsome Thing, a thin shirt only between him and its fang. Cousin William related how the man described the stillness of the night; his horror of a puff of wind, of a falling leaf or twig, and his dread of the approach of animal or bird which might startle the Thing. Then the breaking of dawn, and the twitterings and callings, and all the rousing of the bush. He was afraid lest his horse should come and sniff, and yet longed that it might come, as perhaps the noise might frighten the Thing away. And as the light grew he saw that there were soldier ants close by, and knew that if they crawled on him he must let himself be stung till it should please the Thing to move. He studied the flat head of the Thing and its triangular markings, and thought he must go mad. At last, when the sun was high the snake uncoiled itself and crawled away. And the man got up, shaking as if with palsy. "And Lord," added Cousin William, "you wouldn't have known that chap when he got to the diggings next day. He was trembling all over and couldn't sleep for weeks. And as for his nerve, which was like iron before, it clean broke into little bits."

.   .   .   .   .

"It's only some magisterial business," says Terry, getting up. "I'll be back in five minutes," and presently he is heard calling, "Bring me a Bible, dear," and young Marge runs off with the Bible, remarking, "Some of the Free Selectors come to swear."

When they had "sworn" and gone, Terry explained the matter. "You see, the conditions of their being allowed to own their 160 acres—or less, according to what they take up—are that they must reside on the selection for five years, but most of them after they have put up a hut, leave their wives and children to fulfil the residence condition, and hire themselves out on the job. Then they must pay sixpence a year—five sixpences in all—and must make improvements up to the value of ten shillings an acre, and at the end of the five years they have got to bring along two witnesses and swear before a magistrate to the residence and the improvements, after which they can get a free title. That's what those fellows were doing."

"Seems an easy way of becoming a landed proprietor," said Rothwell, the English boy.

"If they want to become bigger landed proprietors still," says Terry, "they can lease extra land up to two thousand acres, at a rent of threepence per acre; only, to fulfil the residence conditions, it must be within fifteen miles of the original selection. They must put a fence round the extra bit within four years, and when that's over, they can buy it at a price fixed by the Land Board."

Fulvia came along the verandah carrying a silver tray and the tea-pot, Marge and Mena following with cakes and grapes. The lace frills of Fulvia's pretty blouse were tucked up towards her shoulders.

"Please forgive my bare arms. They've been up to the elbows in flour. I'm making bread." Fulvia was very hot, and very tired, though she contrived to look remarkably dainty in her white cooking apron.

Three days ago Fulvia's cook and parlourmaid had found themselves in bad health and requested to be driven to the Doondin terminus. Then it was suggested that the three M.'s should forage among the Selections and see if they could find any one willing to make the bread and wash for Murrum station.

They make quite a colony, the Selectors, along this side of the river, and slab cottages climb up the slope where scrub used to be. All the wilderness of the river is gone. There are millet and lucerne and Indian-corn patches by each bank, and men were ploughing as we passed. The ti-trees have lost their beauty. Of the two great cedars on the Mulgam flat under which we used to boil our afternoon tea, one has been felled and the other is naked and dead; and there are deep wheel tracks down to the arum pool where the Selectors' water-carts go to be filled. The settlement having got the number of children required by administrative powers, and having built the school-house with the cracked bell, which is planted lower down among the gums, the government provides at a stipend of £80 a year, a schoolmaster, who lives in a weather-board hut on the border of the scrub. The debating club sits too in the school-house; there the balls take place, and the Sunday services, when a clergyman comes along; and there the election meetings are held. On the whole, the community seem to have a pretty lively time.

Mr. Hindmarsh, whose wife Fulvia considered a hopeful resource in emergency, was at work among his crops by the creek.

"And how are you getting on with your maize, Mr. Hindmarsh?"

"Bad, bad," answered Hindmarsh, mournfully. "Three hundred bags."

"Done well, ?" asked the doctor. "Tenpence halfpenny, eh?"

Elevenpence," returned Mr. Hindmarsh. "Times are wretched. It ain't only the squatters that has got cause to complain. What the country's coming to I dun-'now."

"It's bimetalism that's at the root of everything," said the man from the next station, "and until silver is acknowledged payment again, and forty shillings instead of twenty given to the pound, the country will never come to any good."

Mr. Hindmarsh couldn't see how that could make a difference, and another Selector called Bascomb, who seems a serious person, and is, I hear, chief spokesman at the debating - society meetings, disagreed with him.

"You see, it's this way," said Mr. Bascomb. "If all the produce in the world was put on this side" (prodding the ground with the butt of his bullock whip), "and all the gold in the world was put on the other side, why, there wouldn't be gold enough to buy the produce. For those that have the gold it don't matter ; and for those who haven't it's a bad job."

"That's about it," said the man from the next station.

Mr. Hindmarsh changed the conversation. "My word! it's been terrible hot to-day. . . . The missus did you say? *I* dun-'now. Most like you'll find her up yon'." His long upper lips puckered down over his teeth; and he jerked his thumb in the direction of a slab house with a verandah, set in a garden of stumps and some pumpkin vines, on the side of the hill.

Fulvia felt a delicacy in pressing inquiries. Hindmarsh was known as "a quiet man but given to sulks, and awful bad to put up with." His neighbour Garstin, who was helping him, was loud and masterful, and only that morning Garstin, up at the station on business, had related how the Hindmarshes had had a difference, and had given it as his opinion that a chap "mum in his tantrums" like Hindmarsh was more aggravating to a female than the most raging of devils, and that, therefore, Mrs. Hindmarsh might not be unwilling to distract her thoughts by a day's baking. "But Lord! I says to Hindmarsh," continued Garstin. "You doan't know how to take the women, Hindmarsh. Why, you mun give 'en a kick and knock 'en down, and they'll coom all right after a time or two. Doan't crush 'en with silence"; which became a family saying at Murrum, and when any one nursed his grievance in dignified aloofness it was customary to remark, "Doan't crush 'en with silence."

Mrs. Hindmarsh, who is a big woman with great black eyes and crinkly hair, did not look in the least crushed, as she came up from the pumpkin patch with a huge pumpkin under one arm and a baby under the other. She had got a batch of bread coming out of the oven that very minute, she said, and if we liked we could take it over.

"I am ashamed to ask you into such a dirty place. I've been cleaning after the rains. The bread don't look as nice as it might, for it's baked in a camp oven; if there's a cake-tin or two to spare at the station I'd make the loaves a better shape for the table. . . . No, I wouldn't come to do the washing at the station, you'd best get some one else—there's Mrs. Garstin perhaps—but *I* don't know. . . . You've had a deal of trouble I hear in the kitchen. If you want your moleskins washed, Mr. Rothwell—or the doctor—tell him I'll do 'em if you send 'em over. There's funny things goes on in the kitchen with them girls, ain't there, Mr. Rothwell?"

" There's plenty of funny things in Australia, seems to me, Mrs. Hindmarsh."

" Yes, they're queer, those servant girls. They objected to the moleskins. I heard the word; you send them over, Mr. Rothwell."

" Well, if you've time, Mrs. Hindmarsh."

" Oh, I'll make time—at threepence the pair. . . . So Hindmarsh is going to take a job with the cart up at the station? "

Mrs. Hindmarsh was informed that such was the arrangement.

" Hindmarsh hadn't always come down to going out on the job. We were in South Brisbane once, in a house of our own; it's the bad times has brought us low. He has lost £800, has Hindmarsh." And Mrs. Hindmarsh announced the fact as cheerfully as though she were putting forward a claim to distinction.

We made a little round of calls that afternoon.

Rothwell and Meg had already established friendly relations with the Selections, and had brought a camera, which hung on the pommel of Meg's saddle.

"We've got two plates left, Mrs. Garstin, and Mr. Garstin says he'd like you and the little girl to be taken ; and we'd like to photograph the. house if we may."

"Garstin said as he'd like the two children done," said Mrs. Garstin. "It's seventeen year now since I was took—didn't like to, somehow. But I'd be pleased to have the children. Garstin, he wanted to have little 'Liza done last year, but I said (with a smile at the infant), wait a bit and get in two of 'em."

Mrs. Garstin was the mother of a large family. The doctor joined us while the photographing was going on, and Mrs. Garstin had much domestic intelligence to communicate.

"Jimmy was nearly dead, doctor, since you was here last. Johnny come down from the Scrub and says, 'Mother I want some eucalypty stuff.' 'What for ?' I says. 'Jimmy's had a hurt,' says he ; and sure enough there was Jimmy lying onsensible. . . . But I'm that used to their getting hurts, I don't feel frightened. There was Jo broke his leg, and I pulled the bones together, and bandaged it, and set it in splints ; and the doctor there told me he couldn't have done it better himself. . . . Lift up yer trouser, Jo, and show the doctor and the ladies your leg. . . . And there was Harry as chopped off his fingers—two of 'em hanging by a bit of skin ; and Garstin says, 'Give us a pair of scissors, and have done with 'em.' But I says, 'No, I aint going to have my boy short of fingers if *I* can help it.' So I sets the fingers back again, and binds them up; and they're as good as the others this day. Show the doctor your fingers, Harry. And I had to go to Murrum station for sticking plaister and hump him all the way; and Lor'! I don't know how I done it!"

.   .   .   .   .

After the rains came a great freshness. Higher up the Ubi is a gorge where in old days we always rode after rains to see the spring swollen into a waterfall. There was a question whether the river would be crossable—it was still a brown, turbid torrent. "I don't think we can manage it," said the man from the next station.

Cousin William spurred his horse on. "Keep up," cried Terry.

But Cousin William got through all right, and the rest followed, even to little Mena in her holland knickerbockers, riding man-fashion. The horses swayed unsteadily with the current. The little one couldn't guide hers, and he went down slantways with the stream.

"Baby, keep up," screamed Fulvia. "Keep up, baby." Then Cousin William dashed back and took hold of Mina's bridle, turning her up-stream.

"You should never shout to any one in a flooded creek," said the doctor. "It makes a fellow lose his head—like the mailman on the Jerra the other day, who was as near as possible carried down. They kept calling out from the bank, 'Keep up! keep up!' till the chap trembled and turned white, and at last got so confused that he let the reins drop helplessly and said, 'Which *is* up? I can't tell.'"

We follow a creeklet fringed by she oaks, and bordered on each side by stony ridges. On the top of the ridge, the dark, distinctive line of scrub stands up like a wall from the blady grass and bracken. By-and-by the ridges swell into high hills and come close, blocking the foreground as the valley narrows. The she-oaks thicken, and the whispering among their needle points sounds fuller. There is a great side cleft in the hill, and a white torrent comes foaming down among the grey-black boulders which are scarred and patched with lichen. Terry and Cousin William drag logs and make a bridge over the torrent, the horses are hitched up, and the glen swallows those of us who walk foremost.

It is just a chasm torn out of the mountain side. The grey walls of rock overhang it, making jagged ledges, from which drop ferns and rock lilies—I remember the lilies' feathery plumes in spring, but they are not in bloom now—and there are thick withes of hoya festooning the cliff. High on the top, native bears and opossums and wallabis have their unmolested dwellings. Slanting outward from the cliff are slim trees of the red-barked mahogany, and of mountain ash, as well as a fleshy-leaved shrub giving out an aromatic perfume. Down in the bed, the torrent roars along the channel it has cut, over worn stones and between great grey rocks. It rushes out of a deep pool, dark, mysterious, and still, except where another stream, falling from a gully at a higher level, churns the pool into brown foam.

This is not much of a waterfall. The children climb up the rock ledges close to the fall, and are wetted by its spray. And then there is a rare clamber to the upper ravine, sacred to the memories of twenty years back ; and young Marge comes down presently, her arms full of native geranium and red berries off those same plants from which we elder ones used to gather them long ago.

So we went back to the old scenes—went back to the old scenes !

Do we ever, indeed, get away from the old scenes ?

THE LAST CRUISE OF JOHN MAUDSLEY RECRUITER

BY LOUIS BECKE

THE LAST CRUISE
OF JOHN MAUDSLEY, RECRUITER

BY LOUIS BECKE

THE *Montiara*, barque, of Sydney, from the New Hebrides to Samoa with a cargo of black labour, was lying becalmed upon a sea of glass, with the pitch bubbling up between her deck seams. Ten miles away to the eastward the verdured slopes of two islands—Fotuna and Alofi—which, an hour before had shone a vivid and enchanting green, were now changing to a dulled purple under the last rays of an angry, blood-red sun.

As four bells struck, John Maudsley, the chief mate came up on deck from the main hold, and walking quickly aft, joined his captain on the poop.

"Packenham," he said wearily, as he took off his broad straw hat and fanned his heated face, "there's another poor devil just pegged out—one of the Santa Cruz boys. Thirteen in twenty-one days ! and unless we get a breeze soon they'll begin to die like rotten sheep. Look here, old man, it's no use talking, we *must* let a batch of say thirty up on deck at once—it will at least give the rest some more air."

The two men looked into each other's faces for a few moments in silence, then Packenham spoke.

"It's terribly risky, Maudsley. There are only three sound men in the ship besides you and I, and it would simply be asking those Tanna and Pentecost niggers to cut our throats and take the ship. What chance should we have, old man, with even only a dozen of them if they knew our weakness! Can't you get the sick men to come up on deck?"

"No. They are sulky and savage, and would rather die down there of suffocation. There are now quite half-a-dozen of them sickening. Tried to get one fellow up on his feet, to bring him on deck, but his countrymen looked so threateningly at me that I had to desist."

"Any of the Tanna and Pentecost boys sick yet?"

"No; it would be a damned good thing for us if they were. They're the crowd who are bent on mischief. So far, only the Banks' Islanders have been attacked, and they are the least dangerous of the lot. Something must be done, Packenham. Always thought measles was a baby's complaint, didn't you? I say, old man, look out for the deck for a bit and send for some coffee. I've got a bit of a twister coming on. Oh, this is a lovely trip! all hands but five down with fever, measles among the 'cargo'—the greater portion of which is only waiting its chance to cut our throats; and a blarsted, furious calm to boot."

"Steward, bring some coffee, quick," cried Packenham, as Maudsley, with chattering teeth and shaking limbs crawled up between the up-ended wings of the skylight, and drawing his knees to his chest, lay down on his side, whilst the captain hastily covered him with rugs and blankets until the ague fit was past and the bone-racking agonies of the fever began.

The steward brought the coffee, and Maudsley raised himself on his elbow and caught sight of his captain standing over him.

"Damn you, Packenham, what the devil are you doing here?" he chattered in querulous, irritable tones; "I'm all right. You go and get that 'tween deck ladder up—if the niggers mean to make a rush *one* man with a gun won't stop 'em. Take a look below first, and see what they're doing. If it wasn't murder to do so in such weather, I'd clap the hatches on."

The skipper of the *Montiara* was well used to his mate's language, for the two men were old and tried comrades; and in all matters concerning natives, Packenham always gave way to his subordinate; for Maudsley was not only his chief officer but "recruiter" as well, and no man who ever sailed the Pacific had a greater knowledge of native custom and character nor had displayed it so often in the face of the deadliest danger.

Packenham walked along to the main deck and looked down the hatchway, but the fast gathering darkness prevented him from discerning more than the recumbent figures of his "cargo," with here and there the gleam of a surreptitious pipe or a cigarette of negrohead tobacco rolled in a dried banana leaf. A sailor, armed with a revolver and cutlass, was pacing to and fro across the for'ard end of the hatchway, and presently Packenham motioned him to haul up the light ladder. This was done without noise; and then the captain went to the deck-house, and, putting his head in at the door, addressed the occupants (six hands) which it contained.

"Here, I say you fellows, can't you shake off a bit

of fever ?   Why, there's the mate, who is worse than any of you, and whose teeth are going like a cotton-gin at full speed, dancing a jig on the poop to himself. Come, buck up my lads."

The boatswain, a tall, sallow-faced Maori half-caste, crawled slowly out of his bunk.

"I'm feeling a bit more fit, sir. I can take the wheel, if a breeze comes, if I can't do anything else."

"That's right, Bill. Here, strike a light first and let me look at you fellows. Steward looking after you all right, eh ? "

" Yes, sir," answered one of the men with a groan, " we has got all we wants, sir ; but we doesn't like bein' here by ourselves. Tommy Samoa there "— pointing to a native seaman lying on the deck of the house rolled in a mat—" says that if those Tanna men make a rush all us chaps will have our throats cutted and will be blue sharks' meat afore we knowed where we was."

" Just what Maudsley said," muttered Packenham to himself, then he added aloud, " You needn't be scared ; the hatchway ladder is hauled up and there's a man on the lookout, not ten feet away. Have you your arms by you ? "

" Yes, sir."

" Well, what the blazes are you making a song about ? You stand a better show in a good, strong deck-house than do the rest of us."

Then raising the lamp he surveyed the place, examined the men's carbines and pistols, and then went on his usual nightly round along the deck of the disease-smitten ship. Ten minutes later he rejoined Maudsley, who was now sitting up, clad only in his pyjamas, and pressing his throbbing head between his hands as the fever heat ran fiercely through his boiling veins.

"Pack.," he began excitedly, "there's a bit of an air up aloft. Look over the side and you'll see we're moving. Does she steer, Harry?"

"No sir, not yet," answered the helmsman.

Packenham looked aloft and then over the side.

"You're right, Maudsley, a breeze is coming sure enough, and a breeze means everything to us; we can run into Singavi Bay on Fotuna. One of the two French priests there is a doctor, and we can put the sick people ashore at any rate."

Maudsley gave an irritated laugh.

"Don't be a fool. I know you're not a brute; but why the —— don't you think of what you're saying? There's a thousand natives on Fotuna, and it would be a damned dirty thing for us to do to dump these measly brutes of ours among them. If we did, the chances are that there wouldn't be another native left alive on the island in a month. . . . Now, this is my idea: if we can get up under the lee of Alofi, we can anchor. There is no one living there— at least not that I know of—as the island is only used by the Fotuna people for their yam plantations, and they seldom go there. There's good holding ground under the west point— ten miles away from Fotuna."

Packenham nodded.

"I see; go ahead."

"Well, as soon as we get there, let us land the whole lot—Tanna boys, Pentecost boys, and the Banks' Islanders. Plenty of coco-nuts, yams, and taro, and, above all, a fine big stream of running water. They'll be as right as rain there ; and then while you and the hands disinfect the hold and the rest of the ship I'll start off for Singavi in the boat with a couple of hands and see if the French priest— the medicine-man fellow—will come back with me. By God, Pack., he'll have to come. We mustn't let these poor devils die like rotten sheep."

"Look here, Maudsley ; you give the word, and I'll do whatever you say must be done. Hurrah ! here's the breeze now, and no mistake—but nearly dead ahead."

"Never mind that," said Maudsley, languidly ; "we can't pick up the anchorage to-night, but we'll be near enough at daylight. Try and fix that wind-sail, Pack., so that some of this cool breeze goes down into the hold."

Packenham, with the three seamen who were able to work, and the steward, set to and trimmed the sails, and under the bright light of myriad stars the little barque glided over the silent sea.

.   .   .   .   .   .

An hour before the dawn, Maudsley, who was feeling better, had taken the wheel, whilst Packen-ham and the others were ranging the cable ready for anchoring. The clang and thump of the heavy iron links as they fell upon the deck seemed to put new life into the crew, and even those who were lying sick in the house came out into the cooling morning air, and with weakened arms and trembling knees helped to flake the chain along ship-shape.

Just as they had finished, and as the first yellow lights of the rising sun were dispersing the thick mists of Schouten Mountain on Fotuna Island, the steward came softly up to Maudsley and touched his arm.

"The second mate is dead, sir."

Maudsley's hands gripped the spokes of the wheel tightly, and then he ran his eye aloft before he answered.

"Was he conscious, steward?"

"Yes, sir, he was—just at the last. He arst fur you, sir; an' when I told 'im that you was at the wheel, an' the skipper an' the rest of the hands was gettin' ready for anchorin', he says to me, 'Don't call the mate, steward, but tell 'im as there's a letter under my piller for some one as he's a-heard me a-speakin' of.' An' without another word, sir, he turns on his side an' dies nice and quiet."

"All right, steward. Go below and get me a stiff glass of brandy. And, look here, while I think of it, put that letter of Mr. Belton's in the captain's cabin. Hurry up now, you damned Cockney swab, and bring me that brandy—I want it."

The steward disappeared without a word, and soon came on deck again with half a tumblerful of liquor.

The chief mate, his hand now quite steady, took the glass.

"Thank you, steward. You're no Cockney swab, but a good little chap. There's a twenty-dollar gold piece in the top after-drawer of my locker—that's for you. . . . You see I've got the fever pretty bad this time, and as like as not I'll slip my cable—you know what that means, my Borough Road fried-fish-eating friend, don't you, though you're no sailor man? Sometimes it means going to hell suddenly, instead of having a parson to 'ready' you up for it, though as like as not he'll tell you that you'll appear as white as snow before the throne of God. . . . Clear out, damn you! What the devil are you staring at? The skipper will want his coffee presently."

The steward, an under-sized, bent-shouldered old man, placed his hand on the edge of the skylight and looked into Maudsley's face.

"You're very ill, sir—I can see that. Can't I call one of the hands, sir, to take the wheel?"

"No, you can't. Go below and get that twenty-dollar piece and stow it away—and clap a stopper on your jaw-tackle, you silly old fool!"

Presently Packenham came aft and stood beside him.

"We're all ready for'ard, Maudy."

"Right you are, Pack. We'll go about presently; another half hour will bring us close enough, I think, though I can't see where we are very well as yet. Take a cast of the lead, will you, old man, as soon as we are in stays? Oh, God! Look there!" and he sprang down off the poop to the main hatch and tried to beat back the upward rush of threescore or more of naked savages with his clenched fists.

Packenham and the three seamen ran to his aid; and then began a deadly struggle—the white men trying to hurl back the savages into the hold instead of using their revolvers. But in less than ten seconds one of the sailors was thrown down upon his back and his brains dashed out with a tomahawk; then, and not till then, was a shot fired. Packenham was the first to bring his pistol into play, and none too soon, for a huge Tanna man had seized him by the beard with his left hand, and in another moment would have driven a knife into his heart. The sharp crack of the heavy Colt was followed by another and another, and each time a native went down ; then came the loud reports of the seamen's carbines, and the lust of slaughter had seized upon them all, as, flinging aside their firearms, they drew their heavy cutlasses and slashed and cut and stabbed the naked figures of the now maddened islanders. Up to this time not more than thirty had succeeded in actually gaining the deck by means of the ladder they had so cunningly made and placed in position ; and of these eight or ten were lying either dead or dying on the deck, as many more had been hurled below, and the rest, when they saw Packenham cut down two of their number and the boatswain smash the skull of a third with the butt of his carbine, turned and fled for'ard. Some of them ran up the forerigging, and these were being picked off one by one by Tommy Samoa and the other seamen, when Maudsley struck their weapons from their hands, and fiercely bade them cease such useless slaughter.

"On with the hatches," he said pantingly, as he stooped over the coamings and pulled up the ladder the natives had placed in position—a mere bamboo pole with half-a-dozen cross-pieces lashed to it with cinnett—"on with the hatches, men. They'll give in now, but we must take no further risks, and there must be no more of this bloody work."

As the hatches were being put on, Maudsley leant over and looked at the savages below. They had all gathered as far aft as possible, believing that the white men, now that daylight had come, would open fire on them.

Maudsley bade them remain quiet; their lives would be spared, he said, if they obeyed him. Then he called to those of their number who were aloft, and told them to come down and go below. They stared at him sullenly and refused.

"Then stay there, you brutes," he said with a curse; "they can't hurt us, Packenham, up there. Now let us get to anchor."

A cut from a tomahawk had laid open his cheek, and Packenham, who himself had a knife-thrust through the arm, quickly bound it up, and then Maudsley again went aft to the wheel and brought the barque to an anchor under a high-wooded bluff on the western point of Alofi Island, and in water as calm as that of a mountain lake. The bodies of the dead natives were then thrown overboard, and that of the white sailor carried aft and laid beside the second mate's in the cabin.

Then, when those of the crew who had been wounded had had their hurts attended to by the captain and steward, the ensanguined decks were washed down, coffee and biscuit were served out, and Maudsley went for'ard, and again urged the Tanna men who were aloft to come down.

"If we are to die, we can die here," was their sullen answer.

The white man was losing patience; the wound on his face made him feel sick and faint, and a sudden spasm of ague shook his frame. He took his pistol from his belt.

"I promise you that no harm shall be done to you if you come down quickly and go into the hold with your countrymen. Have I ever lied to you?"

"No," replied the oldest man of the four—a wild-eyed, vicious-faced brute, with his hair twisted into countless tiny curls, which hung in a greasy tangle down his neck and cheeks.

"Then do as I bid you, or I shall kill you from where I stand—quick!" and he raised his right hand.

Slowly and suspiciously they descended, still grasping their blood-stained knives and tomahawks. As they reached the deck they stopped and glared about them with the ferocity and fear of hunted tigers.

"Keep back there, men," said Maudsley to the crew who were standing near the main-hatch, "they'll want a bit of coaxing. Hang a line over the for'ard end of the hatch so that they can get down." Then putting his revolver back into its pouch, he unbuckled the belt and laid it down on the windlass.

"Now, come with me, men of Tanna," he said quietly, "no one shall hurt you. See, I hold no weapon in my hand, and the rest of the white men, too, have laid down their guns." Beckoning to them to follow, he walked to the hatchway, then turned and faced them.

"Now listen. Take hold of that rope and go down one by one. And tell your countrymen and the men of Pentecost that if they sit down quietly till the sun is high in the sky they shall have food and water given them. Then when all the badness is out of their minds, they shall come on deck, ten at a time, and the smell of blood will no longer be in our nostrils. But before food and water is given, every knife, every tomahawk and every club must be brought on deck to me by two men. Now give me these,"

and he reached his hands out for the weapons they
themselves carried.

Two heavy butcher knives and one tomahawk
were, after a little hesitation, given up, were at once
thrown over the side, and the three disarmed savages
went below ; the fourth man—he with the greasy
curls—still clutched his tomahawk tightly.

"Come, be quick," said Maudsley, give it to me."

"Take it, white man !" and the native swinging
the keen-edged weapon swiftly above his head, struck
it deep into the officer's side, and with a yell of
triumph he sprang over the side and swam for the
shore—only to throw up his arms and sink as Packenham sent a bullet through his head, before he was
fifty yards away from the ship.

   .   .   .   .   .   .

"I'm done for, Packenham, old man . . . No, don't
carry me aft, time's too short. There's a letter for
poor Belton's girl, Pack., which you must give to her.
Tell her she must forgive me for tempting him to ship
on this cruise—my last cruise, old man."

Very gently they lifted and carried him aft and
quickly rigged an awning, for the sun was blazing hot
and fiercely upon the vessel's decks. Then Packenham, with the quick-falling tears coursing down his
bronzed and bearded face, knelt beside the dying man
and took his hand.

Maudsley opened his eyes and smiled at his captain
and gave a faint answering pressure. "Don't you
worry, old fellow. Somehow I don't much care. But
it was hard for poor Belton to die—he was a bright
young shaver, and a gentleman. I've got my gruel

this time, and I'm not going to make a—song over it. And I'm no loss to any one."

Then in slow, laboured words he told Packenham what should be done. The sick natives should be put ashore as soon as possible ; the rest disarmed and kept confined till aid could be obtained from the white traders on Fotuna, who would find him native sailors to help sail the barque to Samoa. Nothing escaped him, nothing was forgotten in his seaman's mind that bore upon the ship and her safety.

" How does she lie, old man ? " he asked presently.

" Snug as possible, Tom," answered the captain brokenly.

" Plenty of room to swing if the wind comes from the westward ? "

" Plenty. Tom, old man, I've sent the boat to Singavi for the French priest. She should be back by noon."

Maudsley shook his head. " I don't want any doctoring, Pack. That buck sent it home properly." Suddenly, by a mighty effort he half raised himself.

"Steward, boatswain, come here ; I want you fellows to witness that I have said that all the money coming to me for this cruise is to be paid to Captain Packenham." Then he sank back again, and motioned to the captain to come closer.

" Pack.," he whispered, " send it all to Belton's girl."

Packenham bent his head, and then Maudsley the Recruiter gave a long, heavy sigh and closed his eyes —his last cruise was ended.